Treasure at Morning Gulch

by Joan Rawlins Biggar

Illustrated by Kay Salem

Publishing House
St. Louis

Scripture quotations in this publication are from The Holy Bible: NEW INTERNATIONAL VERSION © 1973, 1978, 1984 by the International Bible Society. Used by permission of Zondervan Bible Publishers.

Copyright © 1991 Concordia Publishing House
3558 S. Jefferson Avenue, St. Louis, MO 63118-3968
Manufactured in the United States of America

Library of Congress Cataloging-in-Publication Data

Biggar, Joan Rawlins, 1936–
    Treasure at Morning Gulch/Joan Rawlins Biggar.
        (Adventure quest)
    Summary: Twelve-year-old Jodi finds adventure and spiritual enlightenment when she, her brother, and their cousin discover an abandoned gold mine in Washington's Cascade Mountains.
    ISBN 0-570-04193-7
    [1. Buried treasures—Fiction. 2. Adventure and adventurers—Fiction. 3. Interpersonal relations—Fiction. 4. Christian life—Fiction.] I. Title. II. Series: Biggar, Joan Rawlins, 1936– Adventure quest.
PZ7.B483Af   1991
[Fic]—dc20   90-2440
                                                                    CIP
                                                                    AC

1 2 3 4 5 6 7 8 9 10   00 99 98 97 96 95 94 93 92 91

To my parents
who made my adventures possible
and to Marcella
who shared many of them

Contents

Off to Morning Gulch

Jodi Marsh bounced excitedly as the evergreens on either side of the road got bigger and taller. In the back of the truck with her and Mike and their cousin Billy Skarson were the backpacks for their hike to Morning Gulch. Ever since she'd heard about the old mines in the gulch, she'd longed to go there. And now they were actually on their way.

Jodi got up on her knees to peer through the open pass-through window of the pickup's cab. "Turn right at the next dirt road," she heard her father say to Uncle Will.

"Oh, Dad! Do we have to stop at the cabin?" asked Jodi.

Her teacher father turned around and grinned. "Won't take more than a few minutes to check on how things survived the winter, Miss Impatience."

The truck bounced over the uneven road. "It's this next clearing, Will," said Jodi's mother, who was squeezed between her husband and her brother in the cab. As the truck slowed and turned, Billy's big brown mutt, Thunder, leaned so far over the pickup's side that he nearly fell out. He gave a surprised "Woof!" and sat down hard on Jodi's feet.

Jodi pushed him off and leaned out herself to look at the summer cabin. Her heart sank.

"The window's shattered!" she heard her mother cry. "Somebody must have broken in."

The four Marshes hurried to the cabin, followed by Uncle Will and Billy. The culprit, they soon discovered, was not a human intruder. Sometime during the winter, a windstorm had sailed a branch through the cabin window. Then rain blew in to soak rugs, curtains, and wallpaper. Little woods creatures crept in to look for treats.

"What a mess!" groaned Mom, picking up some wrapperless tin cans from the floor.

"I'm afraid repairs can't wait," said Mr. Marsh. "I'm sorry, kids. I know how much you wanted to go on this hike."

Jodi felt like crying. What else could go wrong with this summer? First Dad announced he must spend the vacation working on his master's degree, which meant Mom had to take a job to help with family finances. Next old Eliza (the station wagon) broke down. Jodi's hopes for the usual summer's fun in Washington's Cascade Mountains seemed dashed.

Then a week ago, Billy and Uncle Will arrived unexpectedly from Montana and moved into the basement apartment. Suddenly a summer at home in Bayview looked more interesting, even though she scarcely knew plump, bespectacled Billy. She and Mike had not seen their cousin since his mother's funeral two years ago.

This morning's spur-of-the-moment excursion to the mountains had sent Jodi's spirits soaring. Now her happiness fizzled away like air from a leaky balloon.

"I wish we could go to the gulch," Mom said, "but it will take the whole weekend to put this mess to rights." She scooped up baking powder and dried beans spilling from the cupboard in the kitchen alcove.

Then Jodi had her great idea.

Ever since she could remember, her family had spent summers at their mountain cabin. She and Mike had often gone hiking alone, though never overnight. And ever since Dad told them about the old mining site of Morning Gulch, Jodi'd dreamed of seeing it for herself.

Jodi voiced her thoughts, and she and Mike and Billy held their breath while Dad pondered her proposal. He looked from Mom to stocky, slow-spoken Uncle Will. They both nodded.

Finally he spoke. "We know you've been waiting all school year to get into the mountains. This may be your only chance. Yes, I think we're willing to let you try it."

Jodi squealed. "Really, Dad? We can camp in Morning Gulch by ourselves?" She flung herself at her father. Her enthusiastic hug almost knocked him off the arm of the couch.

Mike and Billy joyfully punched each other's shoulders.

"Take it easy, all of you!" Alan Marsh's eyes, gold-brown like Jodi's and her brother's, twinkled. "Mike's

9

fifteen now. He's responsible for his age—you are too, Jodi. Even if you do tend to knock people off their feet!"

"Oh, Dad! I'm sorry. It's just that I'm so excited!" For the thousandth time, Jodi wished she could be more cool and collected.

Dad continued. "If no one's cleared the trail, you might not be able to go all the way to the gulch."

"If we can't, we'll come back," said Mike. Billy, going on thirteen like Jodi, nodded his red head.

"Another thing. I want your word that you'll stay out of any old mines you might find."

Jodi gave her pledge without hesitating. No dark, spooky, closed-in tunnels for her, thank you.

Mike raised his right hand. "I promise."

"Me too," Billy echoed.

"Get your things together then," said Dad. "I've still got to go back to town for window glass."

Their sleeping bags and extra clothing were already in their packs. Mike slipped a hatchet through a loop on his pack and tied on a coil of rope.

The food was in Dad's pack. Mike took out enough for the three of them. "Here, Jodi," he said in his best take-charge voice. "Put some of this food in your pack, and I'll take the rest. Since Billy's never backpacked before, he shouldn't carry anything extra."

"Bossy!" Jodi grimaced at her lanky brother. She dumped the food into her pack and added a plastic groundcloth.

But even Mike's sudden attack of brotherly authority couldn't dampen her happiness. She laced up her boots and put the little camping Bible, in its waterproof case, into her pack.

"Okay, guys. I'm ready."

"Do you have your jackets?" Mrs. Marsh asked.

"Yes. Oh, my hiking hat!" Jodi clamped a battered sailor's cap over her dark curls.

"Remember, Billy's used to prairies, not mountains. And Jodi, your brother's in charge. Pay attention to what he says."

"I will. I will."

"We're forgetting something." Dad held out one hand to Billy, the other to Jodi. The others linked up in the circle. Jodi saw Billy's puzzled look as Dad bowed his head and began to talk to the Lord. She felt a little embarrassed, but glad too, that Dad had included the Skarsons in their family ritual. ". . . and God," he continued, "we ask you to watch over the kids and keep them from harm. Amen."

"Amen!"

The boys scrambled into the bed of the pickup; Jodi into the front with her father and Uncle Will. Billy's gangly legged dog, of definitely unplanned ancestry, danced nearby at the end of his rope like a noisy kite in a windstorm.

"Wait! We're forgetting Thunder."

"Will he stay with you?" asked Mr. Marsh.

"Sure. C'mon, boy." Billy hefted himself back over the side of the truck and untied his pet.

"Did anybody get the map?" called Jodi. She bounced out of the cab and dashed to the cottage. Grabbing the map from the porch, she ran back to the truck.

"All together now?" chuckled her dad. "We're off!"

Several miles later, the truck rolled slowly along a logging road. Jodi hung out the window, peering down an embankment into a shady hollow carpeted with evergreen needles.

"Whoa. We passed it!" she shouted.

Her father backed the truck to a weather-beaten signpost nearly hidden in salmonberry brush. An arrow beneath the carved words "Morning Gulch" pointed into the hollow.

"Where's the trail?" asked Uncle Will.

"We'll find it," answered Mike. "If we can't, we'll hike back to the cabin."

"We'll see you tomorrow afternoon then, if not sooner." Dad handed them a couple of flashlights from the glove compartment. "Have fun and God bless. Remember, I'm trusting all of you to use good judgment."

The pickup disappeared in a cloud of dust. Jodi tucked her flashlight into her pack. She thrust her arms through the straps and hitched it to her shoulders.

We're really on our way to Morning Gulch, she thought happily. She pushed away a nagging little worry about the unused trail. What could go wrong on a beautiful afternoon like this?

"Let's go!" Mike glanced at the sun. "It's nearly two o'clock."

They shoved through the salmonberry bushes and down the bank. Thunder trotted, snuffling, among the tree trunks. Jodi took a deep breath. She loved the musty fragrance of the forest floor.

"You're sure there is a trail? Doesn't look like anyone has ever been here before," said Billy.

"Here it is," she called. A faint depression in the blanket of brown needles led to a streamlet overhung by thick bushes. Mossy poles, side by side, made a make-shift bridge half sunk in mud and water. Beyond it the overgrown trail climbed a steep embankment.

Mike stepped out on the poles. They squished into the mud. Shallow water flowed over their tops.

Jodi hopped safely across. Billy followed, but as he hesitated for the leap across the muddy stretch beyond the poles, Thunder crashed past him.

Billy yelled, his arms windmilling. Mike and Jodi grabbed his hands just as his feet slipped into the muck. Thunder cocked his head and peered down, one ear up and one ear flopping. They pulled. Billy's feet came free, tumbling all three into the brush.

"Did you get mud inside your boots?" asked Jodi.

"No, but Thunder, why don't you learn some manners?" Billy pushed his glasses up his freckled nose and shook a fist at his dog.

Exotic-looking plants with huge leaves and upright clusters of greenish flowers grew along the edge of the bank. Billy reached for a handhold on one of the overhanging stalks.

"Don't touch that!" shrieked Jodi.

Billy jerked his hand away.

"That's devil's club," she told him. "See the spines on the branches?" She gingerly lifted a broad leaf by its edge. The underside was furry with fine thorns. "If you got a handful of those you'd be in bad trouble."

"At least a Montana rattlesnake warns you before it bites!" Billy replied, looking sheepish at his ignorance. "See, I did get a few stickers."

Jodi examined his hand. "Those will be easy to get out. Any deeper and they'd work themselves in and

13

fester." One at a time she picked the thorns from his fingers.

Further along the trail, Thunder dashed ahead to stand on hind legs against a rotten stump and bark. On top, a chipmunk scolded back, his small striped body jerking his indignation.

"Stop it, Thunder!" As Billy stepped off the trail toward his dog, his foot caught in something tangled among the ferns. He bent down to examine it. "Look at this! A bunch of fine wires all twisted into a rope."

Thunder forgot the chipmunk and bounded over to investigate.

Mike kicked the rusty cable. "Been here a long time."

"Maybe the old-timers left it!" exclaimed Jodi, imagining the prospectors and their pack mules plodding along this very trail. They started up a steep slope where a long-ago landslide had sheared off the trees. Thick brush grew over a jumble of exposed rocks and roots. "Now what?" Jodi wondered out loud. Mike slipped the hatchet from its loop and cut stout walking sticks for all of them.

"Use these. They'll help us keep our footing, and we won't get tired so fast."

Mike pushed the brush aside with his walking stick to find the trail. The others forced their way through after him. Branches tore at Jodi's clothing and face.

In places, thickets of thorny devil's club blocked the way. These they circled, tacking back and forth through the brush until they picked up the trail again.

Thunder whimpered.

"Hey, ol' pal," Billy sympathized. "We'll make it.

14

But hiking through sagebrush was a lot easier, wasn't it?"

Finally the brush thinned. Where the trail entered the forest, Jodi and Mike sat down on a log to rest. Billy struggled to catch up. Jodi noticed his face had turned bright red from the exertion. But he didn't complain. He's a good sport, she thought, pleased.

"Sorry, Bill," Mike called. "We'll try to set a slower pace."

Thunder flopped beside the log. Billy threw himself flat on the ground, chest heaving. "No wonder they quit mining around here," he puffed.

"The mines *were* hard to reach," said Mike. "But the miners had a better trail than this. That slide we just crossed took it out."

From their perch, the cousins could see the gravel road far below, winding through evergreen forest. Behind the opposite hill and all around, jumbled snow-capped peaks spread as far as they could see.

The June sun warmed Jodi's face. It lit the giant firs and cedars marching up the ridge behind her. Somewhere over that ridge lay Morning Gulch. There, she hoped, they'd catch a glimpse of the bygone days when hidden mineral treasures lured fortune seekers to these mountains.

She and the boys might even find a lost gold mine!

Thunderstorm

Though they sat in bright sunshine, the shadow of the opposite hill had begun to creep across the floor of the valley. As Jodi watched, a pile of fat clouds spilled over the distant peaks.

Mike frowned as he noticed them. "We might get wet tonight," he worried out loud. "Maybe we'd better start back."

"Oh, Mike, a little rain won't hurt us," protested Jodi. "I don't mind getting damp. What about you, Billy?"

"Whatever," he shrugged. "I'm not in a hurry to fight through that brush again right away."

Mike gave in. "Let's go then."

He loped up the zigzagging trail in a long-legged stride that made the other two scramble to keep up. He stopped at the top of the ridge, digging into his packsack for candy bars.

"Let's see the map," he said.

Jodi found it and spread it out. Mike ran a chocolaty finger along the zigzag line of the trail, stopping where the last zig turned to the left.

"Here we are," he said. "Now we go along the ridgetop, then down to the creek."

Jodi saw how the trail crossed the creek to run back into a cleft in the mountain opposite their ridge. Morning Gulch.

"We can set up camp in the gulch and still have time to look around, if the trail stays this easy and the rain holds off," Mike told the others.

She folded the map and shoved it into her pack. A sudden breeze struck damp against her skin. It ruffled the ferns along the trail. At the same moment a rumble filled the air.

They looked up. The high branches were tossing. Patches of blue between the branches turned gray as they watched. A chill dimness washed through the woods.

"Oh Mike!" Jodi wailed, suddenly frightened. "We'd better go back. There's going to be a real storm!"

"Too late. We'd get wet anyway," answered Mike. "If we're lucky we'll make the gulch before the rain starts. We can wait it out there."

Storms scared Jodi. But she'd talked Mike into continuing the hike. Now she'd just have to trust his judgment.

Along the ridgetop she and Billy jogged to keep up with Mike. They scrambled over downed trees and pushed through brushy hollows. The sky grew blacker. Each new rumble of thunder made its namesake whine and crowd closer against Billy.

Mike took Thunder by the collar, making the dog trot by his side so Billy could cover ground faster. Finally, the trail dropped down the other side of the ridge.

17

Halfway down the trail, a brilliant flash and a deafening crash exploded right over their heads. Thunder yelped and cringed hard against Mike's legs. As if a monstrous water balloon had burst, the clouds let loose.

Everyone huddled together against the trunk of a big fir. Shouldn't be under a tree in a thunderstorm, Jodi thought fleetingly. But they're all so tall maybe lightning won't pick this one to strike. Her heart pounded. God, she prayed silently, protect us. Please!

Great dollops of water splashed from branch to branch to land with drenching force on the shivering foursome. Clap upon clap of thunder clattered and banged.

Rivulets poured from the turned-down brim of Jodi's sailor's hat and down her neck. Water dripped from her nose and chin.

In spite of her fear, Jodi began to feel exhilarated. Nature's moods in the Pacific Northwest were usually placid, but she was throwing an awesome tantrum now.

"There's no place level enough to pitch a shelter here," Mike shouted above the noise. "We'd better just keep going and hope this lets up soon."

He grabbed Thunder by the collar again and pulled him back onto the trail. Billy looked as frightened as his dog. The little group slogged through streams of water rushing down the rutted trail. They struggled to keep their footing.

When the downpour hit, Billy had put his glasses in his pack since he couldn't see through the water on the lenses anyway. Now he stumbled and fell, time after time. On the steeper places he let gravity carry him down on the seat of his pants. Soon he was muddy from head to toe. Even the orangy freckles on his nose were hidden under freckles of mud.

"Poor Billy," thought Jodi. "Bet he's sorry he ever came to Washington."

Gradually the thunder faded. The force of the rain eased. Below them the cousins heard a new sound. Between the tree trunks they glimpsed the creek shown on their map.

The rain had swollen it to a torrent. White water swept over the boulders on which they should have crossed, leaving no way to reach the trail on the other side.

Jodi gulped. This was terrible! Tears and raindrops began to chase each other down her face. She felt miserably wet and cold. Here in the brush they'd never find a place to set up camp, let alone get dry.

Mike looked at her out of the corner of his eye. "Sorry, guys. Guess we *should* have turned back."

Billy, too, looked close to tears, but Thunder, now that the sky had quieted, barked bravely at the rushing water.

"Let's hike along this side of the creek for a while," Mike suggested. "We might find another place to cross."

Jodi brushed her wet hand across her eyes. "Might as well. We sure can't stay here."

Thunder bounded ahead through the tangle of brush along the stream. Wet branches showered cold water down Jodi's neck and pulled at her soggy pant legs.

Finally, climbing over a jumble of boulders, they came to a narrow, rocky beach. A wide log had lodged in the streambed at the far end of the beach. Water foamed over the log to cascade into churning rapids on the downstream side.

"Looks as if someone put that log there on purpose," remarked Billy. Before the others could stop him, he had stepped out upon the makeshift bridge. "Our boots are already wet. Come on, let's wade . . ."

Jodi's breath caught. She froze. Though shallow, the current poured over the log with such force that it pushed high against Billy's shins. Suddenly realizing his danger, Billy tried to turn. His backpack threw him off balance.

His foot slipped over the edge of the log. Horrified, Jodi and Mike watched him fall into the swirling water. They glimpsed helplessly thrashing arms and legs as Billy tumbled over and over down the stream.

Jodi found her voice and screamed. Mike raced over the rocks. She plunged after him, struggling to rid herself of her pack. She tripped and fell to her hands and knees. Regaining her feet, she saw that the current had flung the terrified boy against a big boulder in the center of the creek. He clung with all his might, choking and coughing, as the waves dashed over him and tried to tear his grip loose.

One more leap landed Mike at a spot opposite the boulder. He dropped his pack, yanking free the coil of rope. He tied one end around his waist and tossed the rest of the coil to Jodi. "Fasten that to something—hurry!" he ordered.

Jodi looked around frantically. Her eyes lit on a broken stump, stripped of bark but with roots still secure in the gravel of the creek bank. She passed the

end of the rope around the stump. With shaking fingers she knotted it tight.

She stumbled back over the rocks to the edge of the stream. Mike picked his way out into the frothing water. Thunder trotted anxiously back and forth at the edge. "Hold on, Billy," Mike called.

Billy's freckles stood out against his pale face.

"Keep that rope tight, Jodi," Mike yelled. The current tore at his knees. He struggled to keep his balance.

One more step—he braced himself against a boulder.

"All right, Billy," he called. "Grab the end of my stick and hang on. Jodi, as soon as he has it, you pull on the rope as hard as you can!"

Mike leaned against the rope tied around his waist, reaching out over the rushing water with the end of his walking stick held in both hands. Billy lunged. As he let go of the rock, the current yanked him downstream. Jodi screamed again. Then she saw he'd managed to catch hold of the stick just in time.

Mike fell across the rock against which he'd braced himself. Jodi dug her heels into the gravel and pulled back on the rope with all her strength. Billy pulled himself hand over hand up the stick. Grabbing Billy's jacket, Mike guided his clutching hands to the rope. As Jodi backed up with the rope, the two boys pushed toward shore.

Billy collapsed in a heap among the boulders. He coughed and gagged. Up came the water he had swallowed. Thunder, his tail wagging his whole body, danced circles around the three young people, licking any face he could reach.

Jodi found that she was shaking. No one spoke for several moments. Mike, his voice rough with the sudden release of tension, broke the silence. "Buddy, are you ever lucky! What made you try such a dumb stunt?"

Billy looked utterly miserable. "It—it *was* dumb, I guess. But the water looked so shallow . . ."

"He didn't know, Mike. And scolding won't help. Thank God you had that rope along!"

Jodi felt like saying that if they had followed *her* advice when the storm hit, by now they'd be nearly back to the logging road. Instead she asked, "What are we going to do?"

No one answered. Aside from bruises, Billy was unhurt. The sleeping bag and clothing in his pack were soaked, but his glasses hadn't broken. He shook off the water and put them on. Both boys were shaking with cold.

Jodi stared into the underbrush. Things just couldn't get any worse! Was it only a few short hours ago she had felt that they could handle anything that might happen? If they ever did get home, Dad and Mom would never again trust them to go camping on their own.

The gloom in the forest did not decrease, although the storm had passed. Night was coming. They had to find a place to make camp.

Suddenly Jodi leaped to her feet.

"Look!" she exclaimed.

A Surprise
Shelter

A faint trail led back into the brush. "Let's follow it. It isn't just a deer trail. You can see that it was graveled once!"

Hoisting their packsacks, the boys pushed after Jodi into the dripping underbrush. They could pick out traces of a path among the evergreens beyond. Following these traces, they rounded a clump of spruce trees whose roots straddled a huge rotten log. They stopped short.

Directly ahead, backed up to a tree-filled ravine, stood an ancient log cabin built of hand-hewn logs. Above the heavy door was a window shuttered with cedar planks. Thick moss covered the roof, with huckleberry bushes growing in the moss.

Plainly no one had disturbed the building for many years. Weeds and brush crowded against it, even in front of the door. Rain still dripped from big old cedars around the little clearing.

"Would you look at that!" Mike exclaimed. "Let's see what it's like inside. Maybe we can camp here!"

"B-b-best idea anyone's h-had all day!" Billy stamped up and down, slapping his arms against his body.

There was no lock on the door, but age and moisture had warped it tightly in its frame. All three youngsters put their shoulders against it and shoved together. The door creaked open just far enough for Mike, Jodi, and Thunder to wriggle through.

"What do you think I am, s-sk-skinny?" Billy chattered. Grasping the edge of the door, he pulled it open a few more inches so he could squeeze inside too.

Jodi strained to see in the dimness. A few rays of light filtered through a cobwebbed window at the other end of the room. Mike took the flashlight from his pack and shone it around the cabin.

A crude staircase against the wall to the right of the door led to a loft. Beneath the stairs sat a plank bedframe with slats fastened across it. Against the walls to the left were crude cupboards and a rusty iron cookstove. A homemade table and chairs stood near the small window.

"Strange," said Jodi. "It looks as if whoever lived here left in a hurry. See that old rusty kettle still sitting on the stove?"

"Watch where you step. This floor could be rotten," warned Mike. "Before we do anything else we've got to get warm, or we'll catch pneumonia."

"You're right," said Jodi, aware again of how terribly cold she felt. She slipped off her pack and opened it, glad to find the contents still dry. She checked Mike's pack.

"Lucky you brought blankets, Mike. Billy can wrap

up in one while his clothes dry. His sleeping bag is soaked, so you and he will have to share your blankets tonight." She shook out a rolled-up blanket and handed it to Billy.

As she pulled a change of clothing from her own pack, a folded sheet of plastic fell to the floor. She stared at it.

"If we aren't dimwits!" she exploded. "While we were standing up there on the ridge getting drenched, why didn't someone think of this ground cloth? We could have cut it up to make ponchos."

Mike looked sheepish. "Guess we left our ingenuity at home, Sis!"

Jodi dug deeper into her pack. "I'm going to get into dry clothes. Keep your backs turned for a few minutes." She pulled off her wet clothing. The boys did the same in the shadows across the room.

As she squirmed into dry jeans and sweatshirt and put on sneakers, she felt the chill begin to ease. "Ah, that's better!"

Leaving her wet clothes where she'd dropped them, Jodi cautiously moved across the creaking floor to the old-fashioned cookstove. In the dim light she saw that the woodbox next to the wall still held a few split logs. She found a rusty poker and lifted a stove lid. The firebox was clogged with debris, but worse, big holes gaped in the rusted stovepipe leading to the ceiling.

"We'll never get this stove to work," she said.

Mike carried his boots to the door and emptied the water in them onto the ground.

"It's just drizzling now," he called over his shoulder. "Bring that firewood, Jodi. If I cut away some of this brush we can build a fire out here."

He took his hatchet and began to chop at the roots of some bushes growing in front of the cabin. While he cleared a space down to the dirt, Jodi walked over to the clump of spruce they'd passed earlier. Close to the trunk she found many small dead branches that snapped off easily. The mass of overhanging foliage had kept them dry. She carried an armful back to the cabin.

"Here's our tinder, Mike. You don't think that old firewood is too rotten to burn?"

"We'll have to try it. There's some matches in my pack, Billy." Their cousin, huddled in his blanket, went inside to find them. Jodi arranged a tepee of small dry sticks in the space Mike had cleared.

"Can't you find the matches?" she called.

"Yeah, I found them. And look what else I found. This was on the cupboard." Billy squeezed through the doorway and held out a dented black metal box. He worked the lid off. "See—candles!"

Sure enough, the box was half full of irregularly shaped candle stubs, most of them just a few inches long.

"Good work, Billy! That's a real find! If they aren't too old to burn, we won't have to worry about our flashlight batteries running down!"

Billy beamed, happy that he'd done something right at last.

"Hey, give me one of those candles. We can save some matches too." Jodi struck a match on its waterproof container and lit one of the yellowish stubs. The match sputtered in the misty rain, but the stub burned.

She carefully wedged the candle upright under her tepee of sticks. Soon a thin line of smoke spiraled up. Little flames leaped through the tinder. She added more and larger sticks, until the fire was big enough to kindle the wood from the cabin.

Mike wrapped himself in the plastic ground cloth to protect his dry clothes from the wet brush. He took a pan from the cook kit through the darkening woods to the stream, and brought it back full of water. When the water boiled, they fixed dehydrated soup and hot chocolate, which they took inside to eat. Pilot bread and cheese rounded out their meal.

The cousins ate ravenously. Billy, bundled in his blanket with little more than his orange topknot showing, groaned with pleasure. "Food! For a while this afternoon I thought I'd eaten my last meal!"

"You're not the only one who thought so!" Mike took his wet boots outside. He jammed sticks into the ground by the fire and slipped the boots over them to steam near the heat. He did the same with Billy's boots and Jodi's, and hung Billy's pants and jacket as close as he dared.

He added more fuel. "We'll keep an eye on these things so they don't scorch. Let's hang the rest of our wet things inside and hope they'll be dry by morning."

By now darkness was falling in the clearing. Overhead, silver-rimmed clouds, backlighted by the rising moon, scudded across the sky. Jodi took Mike's flashlight into the cabin and returned with their wet clothing and Billy's backpack.

"Help me wring these things out," she said. "There are some wooden pegs on the walls inside where we can hang the clothes. We can lay the sleeping bag over the table."

Billy had to use his hands to keep his blanket in place, so Mike and Jodi each took an end of his sleeping bag and twisted until the water quit running out. They carried the wrung-out bag and garments inside.

Mike flashed a light over the open shelves above the cupboard. Spying a heavy crockery saucer he lifted it down and set it on top of the sleeping bag as Jodi spread it out. He lit a candle and let some of the wax drip onto the saucer, then set the candle upright in the melted wax.

"That helps," said Jodi. "Can you imagine living with no more light than this at night?"

"They had more than candles," said Mike. He gestured toward a shelf where an old-fashioned kerosene lantern with a cracked glass chimney stood. He picked it up and shook it. "This won't help us though. No kerosene."

They hung the clothing on pegs and over the backs of the chairs. Billy found another saucer and lit a second candle. He squatted by the cupboard and opened the doors. The shelves were empty, except for a stack of musty magazines. Setting the candle on the floor he shook the dust from the top magazine. He turned the brittle, yellowed pages.

"Wow, look at these pictures! Not a photograph in the whole magazine. Just drawings!"

Jodi came to look over his shoulder. He handed the magazine to her and reached for another.

"Did you see the date on this?" she asked in an awed voice. "August, 1910!"

"I wasn't even born then!" Billy exclaimed.

"I should think not!" she giggled. "That was before our grandparents were born. How do you suppose all this has stood here so long without being disturbed?"

"Our map doesn't show the cabin," reminded Mike. "Probably most hikers never knew it was here."

"Even so, in this country buildings fall apart in a hurry if nobody takes care of them."

"This cabin was well built," said Mike. "The roof is steep, so the snow would slide off before caving it in. And I think the logs are cedar. Dad says cedar rots slowly."

Jodi sat back on her heels and ran her fingers through her hair, nearly dry now but tightly kinked from the rain. Her eyes went dreamy as she looked around the shadowy room. What stories these walls might tell, if walls could talk!

Mike interrupted her thoughts. "We'd better figure out where we'll sleep, before the candles burn out." Nothing was left of the one on the table but a sputtering wick about to drown in a pool of wax. He lit another and set it in the same dish.

"Let's see what's up the stairs," suggested Jodi, jumping up.

"Might be a ghost," teased Mike.

"Pooh! There's no such thing." But she let Mike go first up the open stairway.

The candle threw flickering shadows against the wall. The steps creaked. Billy stumbled over the edge of his blanket. "W-wait for me," he quavered.

The stairway led to a narrow landing against the front wall of the cabin. The open sides of the stairwell were guarded by a banister of poles. Mike raised the candle to peer between the uprights. Jodi stood on tiptoe to look, too.

"What do you know!" she exclaimed softly. "A *family* lived in this house!"

An adult could stand upright only under the peak of the roof, which sloped down to the floor at the sides of the loft. At one side stood a bedframe like the one downstairs, only narrower and shorter, and beside the frame stood a child-sized table and chair. Jodi could imagine what a cozy retreat this had been for the child who lived here.

Thunder pushed past Mike and went snuffling about the room. Billy spoke. "See any ghosts?"

Mike laughed. "Thunder will take care of any ghosts. Why don't you bring that flashlight up, Billy?" Mike bent low on the landing to avoid knocking his head on the slanting roof and stepped out into the middle of the room. The others followed.

A small, shuttered window centered each end wall. Jodi walked across the protesting floor to open the back shutters. She flashed the light through the glassless opening. The beam fell on tree tops in the gully below. "Bet there's a nice view from here in the daylight," she called over her shoulder.

"The view can wait until morning," said her brother. "We'd better get to bed if we're going to start back early."

"I'm going to sleep up here," Jodi told the boys.

"Okay. We'll use the candles and you can use your own flashlight. But don't leave it on too long," cautioned

Mike. "I think I'll hang the wet sleeping bag over these railings. That way air can reach it from both sides."

He dragged the bag up the steps and draped it over the angle where the railings came together. Jodi tested the slats on the small bedframe, surprised that they were still strong enough to hold her. They were narrow enough to be a bit springy, and close together. Sleeping there would be much more comfortable than sleeping on the floor.

She heard the boys arranging their blankets downstairs. She unrolled her sleeping bag on top of the slats. Then she sat down on the edge of the bed, stretching her slender legs out in front of her. "Oooh!" she groaned. "I'm sore all over!" She kicked off her sneakers and wiggled her bare toes. Bare toes!

"Mike," she called. "Did you bring our boots in?"

She heard the door scrape open, then shut again.

"Thanks," her brother called back. "The fire's out, so they can finish drying in here."

Jodi squirmed into her sleeping bag, whistling under her breath. "Mom and Dad and Uncle Will are probably frantic if the storm was as bad in the valley as it was here," she muttered. She wished there was some way to reassure them. "We'll just have to get back as early as possible tomorrow. Hope I can get to sleep after everything that's happened today!" She rolled over. "Wish I'd brought one of those old magazines up here to read."

The camp Bible! Jodi remembered putting it in the little pocket in the front of her pack. Pulling it out, she leafed through to Romans, the book she'd been reading in her daily quiet time. Parts were hard to understand, but one verse had caught her eye at bedtime yesterday—was it really only twenty-four hours ago?

Running her finger down the page, she stopped at Romans chapter 8, the 28th verse. "And we know that in all things God works for the good of those who love Him . . ." A few hours ago, when Billy so nearly drowned in the creek, she'd never have believed good could come of that. But God had helped them rescue Billy. Because of his accident, they'd discovered the cabin. Now here they were, warm and dry, when they might have been huddling out under the trees, waiting miserably for morning. "Thank You, God," she whispered.

Jodi flashed the light once more around the little room. The beam slid down the log rafter over her head. Suddenly she bounced upright. Just above the little table beside the bed, something was tucked between the log and the planks of the ceiling.

Scrambling out of the sleeping bag, she pulled a leather pouch from its hiding place. A cloud of dust shook free. Through the leather she felt something hard and lumpy.

Lucy

"Hey, you guys!" Jodi shouted. "I found something!"

"I was almost asleep," Mike called back in an irritated tone. "Can't it wait 'til morning?" But she heard him fumbling for his flashlight, then a thump as somebody tripped on a blanket.

"Girls," grumbled Mike. "Always making a big fuss over nothing."

"Yeah. Girls!" Billy echoed sleepily.

Jodi paid no attention. With trembling hands she loosened the leather drawstring, while her imagination filled the bag with all sorts of treasures.

Her fingers closed around the largest object in the bag. She drew out a funny little wooden doll, about eight inches long, wrapped in a scrap of cloth. She carefully unwound the cloth.

The boys crossed to Jodi and bent to see what she'd found.

"You got us up here to look at a doll?" Billy sounded disgusted, but Mike picked it up and examined it closely.

"Looks like she was carved with a jackknife," he said. "See how the arms and legs are pegged to the body?" The doll's faded hair and features had been drawn in ink. She wore a little red flower-sprigged dress.

Jodi emptied the remainder of the pouch on the table. Out fell some folded papers, a bit of tarnished metal mirror, a few colored rocks from the creek. Last of all, a small glass bottle clunked to the table. Something rattled inside. She picked it up. It felt unexpectedly heavy.

Mike shined the flashlight on it.

They all stared as Jodi worked the stopper free and poured the contents into the palm of her hand.

"It's gold!" she breathed.

They fingered the shiny, roughly-shaped bits of metal with awe.

"I thought gold nuggets were always rounded and smooth," said Billy. "These have pointy, sharp places."

"I thought so too," said Jodi. "But feel how heavy these are? They must be gold!" With care she dropped the glowing bits back into the bottle.

Then she unfolded the brittle papers. One held a child's drawing of a house . . . a square box with a steep roof. In front of it stood a little girl with long braids and an ankle-length dress. At the bottom of the page in careful round letters was written, "Me and Our House."

"That's this cabin!" said Billy. "See the window with shutters above the door?"

"No berry bushes on the roof though," commented Mike.

The second piece of paper held a letter in the same round handwriting. As Jodi studied the faded words, the loft blurred in her mind into the cozy little bedroom of nearly eighty years before. A small girl sat at this very table, a sheet of writing paper before her. She dipped an old-fashioned pen into a bottle of ink and wrote the date at the top, September 3, 1910. Jodi read aloud:

Dear Lottie,

Thank you for seeing us off on the train. Papa met us at the river with two pack mules. I rode on one of them, but papa and mama walked.

We went a long way into the mountins. Mama and I weren't afraid becuz papa was there. Our house is smaller than our house in seattle, my room is upstairs. Papa made my bed and desk.

Thank you for the ribbon you sent for my birthday. We took a picknik lunch to morning gulch. Mama baked a cake with eight candles. We saw where papa works, he is happy becuz he found sum gold.

I helped papa hide the gold until he can take it to be assayed. Tomorrow he is going to blast his mine deeper into the mountin.

Your affecshunit cousin.
Lucy Steincroft

"Pretty good letter for an eight-year-old, even if she did have trouble with her spelling," Jodi commented. She turned the paper over.

"Oh, here's more!" The postscript was smudged, the writing uneven, as if hurriedly done. She read:

Oh, Lottie, yesterday at the mine the dinamite went off too soon. The rock fell on my poor papa. Mama says the mine will be his grave. We are moving to bayside to stay with Uncle Theodore.

Love,
Lucy

No one said anything. Jodi blinked back tears as she slowly folded the papers and one by one put the items back into the pouch.

At last she said, "It seems so real to me . . . as if it happened just yesterday. I wonder what happened to Lucy? I wonder if anyone ever looked for gold here again?"

Billy bounced up and down. "Our folks will never believe this!" he exclaimed. "Wouldn't it be something if we could find the ore Lucy and her father hid?"

Jodi's eyes glowed as this idea took hold. "Oh, yes!" she answered. "What if the gold really was good quality? Maybe we could reopen the mine. We'd all be rich!"

"Hold on, you guys. First we have to find the ore, and she doesn't say where they hid it. And we don't know where the mine was, either."

"Oh, Mike, don't be such a wet blanket!" But Jodi knew Mike was right.

It was a long time before her racing thoughts allowed her to drop off to a sleep punctuated with dreams of tumbling mountain streams and lost mines.

Hours later, Jodi stirred. "Oooh!" she moaned. Eyes shut tight, she stopped in mid-stretch. She felt sore from feet to neck.

Somewhere a liquid melody bubbled up and was answered again and again from points near and far. Jodi opened one eye a little. In a flash, yesterday came back to her.

Daylight flooded through the open window at the end of the room. She slid out of her sleeping bag and hobbled over to it.

Across the gully, rank after rank of dark evergreens climbed a mountain which sloped down to a narrow valley. Jodi could hear the stream plainly through the bird songs vibrating from gully and forest.

She looked to her left, where the gully ran into a straight up and down rockface partly screened by tall firs. "What a beautiful spot Mr. Steincroft chose for a home," she thought.

Jodi shook her sleeping bag, then rolled it up, tucking the leather pouch inside. "Wait until Dad sees this," she whispered to herself. "He'll forget the worry we've caused."

Someone stirred below. Thunder's tail thumped the wall. She called down the stairs, "Are you up, boys? I'm coming down."

"Wait a minute," answered Billy in a sleepy voice. "Let me get my clothes on."

She heard him groan. Sore as she felt, he must feel worse. Thunder galloped up the stairs to poke his cold nose into her hand.

"Ready," Billy called.

Jodi felt of Billy's still-damp sleeping bag on the railing as she cautiously started down. "Oooh-ooh! Are your legs sore too, Billy?"

"I'm sore everywhere. There's a bruise the size of a baseball on my shoulder—I feel like one big bruise all over!"

"Cut the noise. I'm trying to sleep," growled Mike from the corner. Only the top of his tousled dark head showed above the blanket. Jodi winked at her cousin. Tiptoeing over, they each grabbed a corner of the blanket and jerked.

"C'mon, lazy bones, roll out!" Jodi laughed. "The sun's up. We've got lots to do before we start back."

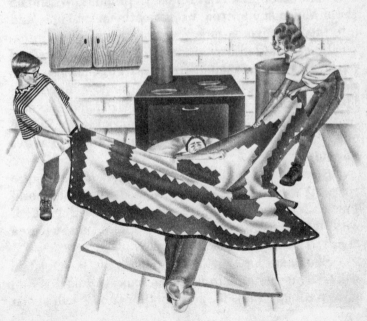

Mike swatted at them, but they dodged away. He reached for his boots. The others put theirs on too.

"Billy's sleeping bag is still wet," said Jodi.

"Take a couple of chairs outdoors. We can spread it to dry in the sun while we fix breakfast." Mike kindled a fire while the others took care of the sleeping bag.

"C'mon, Thunder, let's get some water." The big dog trotted ahead of Jodi down the trail to the stream. During the night the creek had dropped so that the top of the foot log was once more above water. Looking up toward the shining rocks of Morning Gulch, she could hardly resist the impulse to cross.

Back at the fire, she poured some of the water into a second pot and set both near the flames. When the water boiled she stirred instant oatmeal into one, and into the other, cocoa mix.

She sprinkled brown sugar over the tin bowls of cereal and handed them to the boys. "I'm glad the sugar didn't get wet," she said. "I forgot the powdered milk. This might have been pretty unappetizing."

"I was hungry enough to try to cook one of those noisy robins," Billy said with his mouth full. "I won't complain."

After they ate, they carried their dishes to the stream for rinsing. As they finished, they stood and gazed up at the mountain. Somewhere in that gulch was the mine Lucy wrote about. Three pairs of eyes met with the same thought.

"We're so close . . ." began Jodi.

"Seems a shame to not even look," said Billy.

"We'll just have to do it another time." Jodi spoke

reluctantly. "We've got to get home so the folks will know we're safe." With all her heart she wanted to explore Morning Gulch.

"It's still early. I think we could take a quick look."

Jodi looked at her brother, surprised. Usually she was the one to urge Mike to go just a little further. But Mom had said he was in charge. If Mike thought they should do it, she'd not argue!

Hastening back to the cabin they stamped out the embers of their breakfast fire, finished their packing, and hurried back to the foot log.

Billy looked down into the clear water gurgling under the log. He shook his head. "I can't believe this is the same creek that tried to drown me yesterday."

Mike flailed the underbrush on the opposite bank with his walking stick. Droplets showered from the leaves. The foursome pushed their way through the shoulder-high bushes until they came out into open forest again. Beyond the trunks they glimpsed granite boulders, big as cottages. The evergreens gave way to mountain ash and the delicate new leaves of huckleberry brush.

Rocky slopes rose ahead of them and at either side. A few gnarled evergreens clung to the steep sides of Morning Gulch. Wildflowers nodded at their feet. Jodi breathed deeply of the damp, sweet air. "Did you ever smell anything so *new?*" she asked. "Spring has just arrived here."

"Oh, come on!" protested Billy. "School's out. It's summertime!"

"You think so?" she laughed. "Look behind that boulder above you."

Billy looked. "That's snow?" he squeaked.

"Sure is," said Mike. "The higher you go, the later the season. We've climbed quite a distance since we left the logging road yesterday."

"Yes," said Jodi. "And the top of the gulch is lots higher still. The mine could be anywhere up there." She gestured toward the slope rising above and ahead of them to a snow-covered saddle between the peaks. "Mike, didn't Dad tell us once that the pass up there was one the miners used when they first came into this area from the mineral strikes farther east?"

"Think you're right, Sis."

Suddenly something whistled past Mike's ear and splatted against a boulder. Mike leaped to his feet and launched himself at his cousin.

"Hey, Billy, you forgot to wash your face this morning. Let me do it for you." Mike rubbed a handful of snow in Billy's face while Billy struggled and yelled. Thunder's happy barks bounced back and forth across the gulch.

Jodi wandered on up the slope before the boys should decide to make her their target. Picking her way along a rivulet that ran from patches of snow higher up, she glanced across to the other side. She gasped. Oh, could it be?

Several big rocks had blocked it from view while they rested, but now it stood out plainly—a rectangular black opening in the side of the gulch. Last summer's dead grasses drooped over the top of the hole, almost hiding some weatherbeaten timbers. Could this be the lost mine?

In Morning Gulch

Jodi opened her mouth but no sound came. She took a deep breath and tried again; the excitement in her shout brought the boys running.

A few minutes later they stood peering into a tunnel. As her eyes grew accustomed to the blackness, Jodi dropped the hand which shaded them, disappointed. "It's only a prospect hole. I thought it might be Lucy's mine."

Billy looked puzzled. "What's a prospect hole?"

Mike ducked his head and stepped inside. "The miner thought this looked like a good place to find ore. But there was nothing here. He didn't go far, see?"

The shaft ran back five or six yards into the mountain and ended in a solid rock wall. Water dripped from short stalactites on the ceiling. "Come out, Mike. We made a promise," Jodi reminded.

"Well, at least we know somebody did look for gold here," said Billy.

Jodi took off her sailor's cap. She ran her fingers

through her tangled curls. "Yes," she answered. "But who knows where the real mine is?" She scanned the slopes once again. "Oh, look at the shadows! It's mid-morning already. We'd better start for home."

"I doubt it stormed hard enough in the valley to worry the folks," said Mike.

Jodi wasn't so sure. "If it did, Mike, they might not let us go alone again."

"All right, we'll leave."

At the cabin, Jodi ran upstairs to fasten the shutters. She paused to look around. "Good-bye, little room. I know Lucy must have hated to leave you."

The trail up the ridge was still slippery with the mud they'd churned up the evening before. But once on top they made good time and didn't stop until they reached the edge of the old slide. They paused there for a snack.

Billy tossed raisins for Thunder to catch, one at a time. He held one up. "Sit, Thunder. Sit," he commanded. Thunder cocked his head inquiringly, then leaped to snap the raisin out of Billy's fingers. Billy looked sheepish. "He's smart, really. He just wants to do things his way."

They laughed. "C'mon, Billy," Mike said. "Wish he was smart enough to find us an easy way through this brush patch."

Finally they pushed their way up the last rise and onto the logging road. A few minutes later a Forest Service truck rolled around the curve behind them. The ranger at the wheel leaned out his window.

"You the kids that were hiking in Morning Gulch?"

They nodded.

"Your folks called the station a little while ago to tell us you might be in trouble. Can I give you a lift?"

They tossed their packs into the back and boosted Thunder in after them. They clambered into the cab. "Thanks for stopping," said Mike. "We hoped our parents wouldn't be worried. Was the storm bad here?"

"We had a little rain. But the sky got pretty black up in the hills."

The ranger stopped at the lane leading to the Marsh's summer cabin. They hopped out, calling their thanks. As the truck pulled away, they looked at each other.

"I'll bet we're in for it now," said Jodi.

They set off. As they hurried around the last bend in the lane, they saw their fathers just getting into the blue pickup.

"Dad!" called Jodi.

Both men turned, then started toward them. Adele Marsh came around the side of the house. In a moment she had her arms around all three at once. "Thank the good Lord, you're safe! We've been so worried."

Alan Marsh patted his wife's shoulder. "Well, they're grubby, Mom, but they look fine. We'd just decided, kids, that we'd better go look for you. Did the storm miss you?"

Each waited for someone else to speak. Jodi nudged Mike. "It didn't exactly miss us, Dad," he said. "But we did all right. It's a long story."

Over soda pop and hamburgers, the cousins told of their adventure. Jodi launched so enthusiastically into the tale of the cabin's discovery that the grown-ups forgot to pursue the part about Billy's fall into the stream.

She drew the leather pouch from the rolled-up sleeping bag. "Here's something to interest a history buff like you, Dad." One by one she took the items from the bag: the doll, the rocks and mirror, the bottle of nuggets, and the drawing and letter.

The adults examined each object. Her father read the letter aloud, his voice betraying more interest with each sentence. "You've made quite a discovery here, kids! You're forgiven for worrying us!" He stopped and looked sternly at them. "But don't ever forget. Mountain weather can be treacherous. You've always got to be ready for the unexpected."

"We sure learned that lesson, Dad," Jodi nodded.

But Billy was thinking of something else. "You said we'd made quite a discovery, Uncle Alan. Do you mean we might be able to find that mine and get rich?"

His uncle chuckled. "Afraid not. I only meant that this letter is valuable for the knowledge it adds to the history of this region."

"There ought to be a way to find out more," pondered Mike. "Shouldn't there be records of the old mining claims at the courthouse?"

Dad nodded.

"When did the little girl write that letter? 1910?" asked Mom. "Do you realize she could still be alive somewhere?"

Jodi's brown eyes shown. "I'll bet Mrs. Neileson, the librarian, would know how to find out!"

"How?" asked Billy.

"Why, she can show us where to look for information. Besides, she's a real expert on the history of our county. It's her hobby."

"I'm sure she could help," said Mom. "But right now we'd better finish putting the cabin in order so we can start back to town."

On the way back to Bayside, Billy fell asleep, curled up against his dog. Mike and Jodi sat with backs against the cab, each lost in their own thoughts. Jodi heard snatches of the grown-ups' conversation through the open panel of the back window.

"I've been baffled by that boy of mine for two years," Uncle Will said. "He's a smart boy. He ought not to be failing in school. But since his mother died he's only been interested in his pets or in tinkering in the garage with me."

"In the garage?"

"He likes to help with car repairs. He does well, too, for a boy his age."

"The trouble in school is easy to understand, Will," said his sister. "Of course he'd find it hard to concentrate. When his mother died, it probably seemed as if his whole world had fallen apart."

"It seemed that way for both of us. But I think being with your family will make a big difference."

Jodi thought about that. Billy's coming had already changed things for their family. And little Lucy Steincroft may have set in motion more change.

Detectives
at Work

Dad left with his carpool for the university early next morning, and Uncle Will went off to the Bayside Service Center, the auto repair shop he'd just bought. And Mom had gone to her new job at the bakery.

Billy poked his head in the back door. "Hi, Jodi. Could I wash these muddy clothes and my sleeping bag?"

"Sure. Right over here." She opened the bifold doors that hid the laundry area from the rest of the kitchen.

She dipped some detergent out of the big box and dumped it into the washer for him. "Billy, I heard your father say you've been having trouble in school. What subjects are you failing?"

Billy's rosy face flushed redder. "Everything, I guess."

"Reading?"

"I like to read. It's just that I didn't always turn my assignments in."

"Math?"

"Yes, and social studies . . . and English."

"I want us to stay in the same grade. Why don't we see if we can get some seventh-grade textbooks and review last year's work in our spare time this summer?"

Billy looked pained. "Schoolwork in the summer?"

"We could make it fun. Think how awful you'd feel if you got held back."

"I guess it's worth a try."

"Good. We've got a deal!" Jodi left Billy trying to submerge his billowing sleeping bag in the washer, while she got out the makings for tuna-fish sandwiches. The back door opened again.

"Dad! Why are you home so soon?"

"Today is registration day. No classes until tomorrow. I've stood in lines all morning, and I'm famished!"

Jodi hollered up the stairs for Mike. They all sat down at the table and Dad asked God's blessing on the lunch.

"Kids, what do you say we take a bus downtown and check at the courthouse to see what we can find out about the Steincroft claim?"

"Hey, great! Can we go now?"

"Just as soon as we're through with lunch."

A skinny young man with rimless glasses and a droopy mustache took them on an ancient elevator to the courthouse basement, where the records were stored.

"In 1888," the clerk told them, "the Washington Territorial Legislature passed a law saying mining locations must be recorded with the county auditor. Up until then, you see, each group of miners made their own rules and kept their own records. If your mine was being worked in 1910, we should have a record of it."

He led them into a room filled with shelves of leather-bound books. "Do you know when Steincroft filed his claim?"

"No," answered Mike. "He brought his family to the mountains in 1910, so he must have filed before that."

The clerk pushed a rolling ladder to one of the stacks. He lifted down several heavy volumes.

For some time they poured over the pages of small, faded print. "I can't make any sense out of this at all," Billy said.

"Ah! Here's something," Dad exclaimed.

Jodi went to look over her father's shoulder. She picked out the name "Julius A. Steincroft" in the entry to which he pointed.

"The description of this location seems to match what we know about the gulch. He called his claim the 'Morning Mine.' "

The claim was listed in the records for 1909 and 1910, but there was no mention of Morning Gulch after that.

"I'm not surprised," said Mr. Marsh. "The railroad shut down for a few years about then. The mining boom began to falter. Evidently no one else carried on after Steincroft died."

The clerk carried the books back to the shelf. "Anything else I can do for you folks?"

"Thanks. We've found what we wanted to know," answered Mr. Marsh.

Outside, they paused on the courthouse steps.

"We found that there really was a Julius Steincroft, and a mine in Morning Gulch," said Billy. "But where do we go from here?"

"Jodi's idea about the library is the next logical step," replied his uncle. "I need to see what research materials are available here for my university classes anyway. Do you want to talk to Mrs. Neileson while I look?"

The four of them set out at a brisk pace for the library, eight blocks across town. Jodi smiled to see Billy hustling to keep up, shoulders and elbows pumping to propel him along.

"Don't you people ever go anywhere without rushing?" he complained good-naturedly.

Mrs. Neileson was a plump little lady with very short legs, thick glasses, and a bowl-shaped haircut. Mike briefly explained what they knew about Julius Steincroft. Delighted to find someone with whom to share her interest in local history, she beamed at the three cousins.

"We're allowing very few patrons into the archives right now because we're in the midst of putting our old papers and records on microfilm. But I'll make an exception this time. Come along."

She led them through a door with a sign that warned "Keep Out," and down a narrow staircase to the basement. She sat them at a table and brought two thick volumes of early newspapers to them.

"You said the accident happened in the fall of 1910?

These are the two local papers that were being published at that time. Look for mining news, death notices, society notes. If you find nothing, we'll go through some of our other old collections. Handle the papers carefully. They're extremely fragile," Mrs. Neileson said as she hurried off. "I'll be back to see how you're doing."

Jodi pulled one of the volumes to her. The pages *were* brittle, yellowed, the type very small. This might be a long task! For quite some time the only sound in the musty room was the crackle of pages turning and Jodi's absent-minded, under-the-breath whistle. Mike's exclamation startled the other two.

"Here, under the obituaries!" He pointed to a column in a weekly dated September 12, 1910. He read aloud:

Mr. Julius A. Steincroft passed away as the result of a mining accident at his claim in Morning Gulch, in the mountains east of this city. He was 32 years old and was a son of Frederick Steincroft, Esquire. Some years ago he was united in marriage with Miss Emma Barker, daughter of Wm. C. Barker of Littleton, Ohio, who is left with one child, Lucy Steincroft, to mourn his death.

A memorial service will be held on Wednesday this week at 11 o'clock in the North Hill Church.

Mrs. Steincroft and her daughter are in mourning at the T. F. Hinton residence and will reside there for an undetermined length of time.

Just then Mrs. Neileson returned. She leaned over to peer at the notice. "T. F. Hinton! Why he was the owner of one of the town's first sawmills; sold out to Weyerhauser years ago. Hinton Hill and Hinton Street are both named after him!"

"I suppose he died long ago," said Jodi.

"Oh, yes," replied the librarian. "But he had children, and grandchildren. I went to high school with his grandson, Theodore the Third. I believe Ted is an official in a big lumbering company in Portland now."

While Jodi copied the obituary, Mrs. Neileson bustled upstairs. She came back with Theodore Hinton III's address on a slip of paper.

"We just happened to have a Portland directory," she said.

What good fortune! Upstairs, an assistant librarian gave them paper and an envelope.

With the boys' help, Jodi drafted a letter to Mr. Hinton, explaining their discoveries and asking if he could tell them anything about Lucy Steincroft. Each of them signed it.

Then they went in search of Alan Marsh. In excited whispers they told him what they had found and showed him their letter.

He cautioned them not to get their hopes too high. "After all," he said, "it's highly possible that this Mr. Hinton knows nothing of Lucy Steincroft. Or if he does, she may no longer be living."

Nevertheless, on their way to the bus stop, they bought a stamp at the post office and mailed the letter. "Now," exclaimed Jodi, "there's nothing we can do but wait."

Exciting
News

To keep busy while they awaited an answer to their letter, Jodi set up a morning lesson time for Billy. Mike helped with math, and Jodi reviewed his other subjects.

But the little girl of the cabin was never far from her mind, and finally an answer came. She ripped the end off the envelope and read aloud:

Dear Mike, Jodi, and Billy,

I received your letter with a great deal of interest. Lucy Steincroft was my father's cousin. Mrs. Steincroft and Lucy came to live with his family after the mine accident. Several years later, Lucy and her mother returned to Seattle.

Lucy taught school when she grew up. We visited her often when I was a boy. She never married. In recent years she has been in poor health and is now living at the Mountain View Nursing Home in Bayside.

I took the liberty of writing to tell her of your

desire to locate her. I hope you will go to see her. She will enjoy meeting you.

Sincerely,
Theodore F. Hinton III

Jodi's eyes grew round beneath her tousled dark curls. She gave a soft whistle. "So Lucy *is* still alive!"

"Mr. Hinton seems to think she'd like to see us," said Mike.

"But she must be almost ninety," put in Billy. "That's awfully old. How do you talk to someone that old?"

"I suppose just like you talk to anyone else," Jodi answered uncertainly. "We can show her what we found, and . . . and then . . . just ask her questions."

"We ought to call the nursing home before we go," suggested Mike.

They all trooped into the kitchen while he made the call. "The receptionist said this afternoon would be fine," he reported.

"A nursing home's like a hospital, isn't it?" asked Billy. "Maybe I'll just stay home and finish my math."

"No you don't. We're all in this together!" Jodi didn't want to admit it, but butterflies fluttered in her stomach too.

She ran upstairs to splash water over her face and run a comb through her hair. As a second thought, she slipped out of her shorts and T-shirt and put on a dress. Dropping the leather pouch into her old school bookbag, she rejoined the boys.

Scribbling a note to Mom, she propped it against

the toaster on the kitchen cabinet. Then they all hurried off to the bus stop.

The Mountain View Nursing Home was a big white building trimmed with cheerful coral pink. A veranda ran across its front. A few elderly patients sat drowsing there in wheel chairs and rockers.

The building sat atop a ridge, facing Puget Sound and the Olympic Mountains in the west. Toward the east it overlooked the Cascade Range. Many of these big old houses had been built by the early lumber barons, Jodi knew. Perhaps Lucy and her mother came to a mansion like this when they went to stay with her uncle, the first Theodore Hinton.

"Why are you hanging back?" Mike's teasing question jolted Jodi into the present. "You two look like you have stage fright."

"What's there to be afraid of?" she retorted. "Come on!"

She marched up the hillside steps toward the building. As they stepped onto the veranda she paused, wondering whether to walk right in, or knock. A very old man with only a few white hairs on his bald head slumped in a wheelchair a few feet away.

She stopped beside him. "Excuse me, sir. Where can we find the receptionist's office?"

The old man's face twisted into a toothless grin. His head wobbled back and forth as garbled sounds came out of his mouth. He lifted one wavering hand toward the front door. Jodi felt a little frightened, but she forced an answering smile.

"We must just walk in," she told the boys. Mike opened the door, and they stepped into a large room

56

full of sofas and easy chairs, low tables, and green plants. A few residents sat visiting or watching television.

A nurse came to meet the young people. They introduced themselves.

"I'm Mrs. Kratz, the nursing supervisor," she told them. "You will enjoy Miss Steincroft. She's as sharp as a tack in spite of her ailments."

As she spoke, Mrs. Kratz led them briskly down a hall and into a big airy room to a bed at the far end of the ward. White heads and gray turned to watch them pass.

Propped against pillows, a tiny lady wearing a lacy pink shawl smiled a welcome. Strands of yellow-white hair escaped from the knot on top of her head.

Lucy Steincroft stretched gnarled hands toward Jodi and the boys. "You must be the young people Teddy wrote about," she said. Bright blue eyes twinkled from a face as lined as old parchment. "Do sit down. It is so nice to see some young faces."

Mrs. Kratz placed three folding chairs beside the bed.

The old lady opened the drawer in her bedside table and drew out a gold-foil covered box of chocolates. She lifted the cover and offered the box to Jodi. "Wouldn't you like some?" Jodi helped herself and passed the box to the boys. Billy looked from one fancy chocolate to another. "Don't be bashful, young man. Take several."

Jodi bit into her raspberry cream. "Mmmm! Thank you. It's delicious." She looked around as she savored the smooth flavor. Among scraps of cloth on the bedside table sat a baby doll, dressed in bright new clothes.

"Miss Steincroft, did you make that pretty doll dress?"

The old lady chuckled. "Yes, my dear." She reached stiffly for the doll and turned it around for their inspection. "People bring me old dolls they've cleaned up. I sew new costumes and give them to poor children. I'm slow because the arthritis makes my fingers stiff, but I like making the children happy." She spoke in little rushes, as if short of breath. "But you didn't come to hear about my dolls, now, did you?"

Jodi drew a deep breath. "I don't quite know where to begin, Miss Steincroft. My cousin and brother and I started for Morning Gulch two weekends ago. We got

caught in a terrible storm . . ." When Jodi reached the part about discovering the cabin, she took the leather pouch out of her book bag and put it in the old lady's lap.

Lucy's hands shook as she touched it. A faraway look came into her eyes. "I haven't thought of this in years. It was my treasure bag," she whispered. "When I discovered I'd left this behind, I felt heartbroken."

Jodi untied the strings for her, then gently shook the contents onto the coverlet. Lucy picked up the wooden doll.

"It's Lottie!" she said softly. "My father made her for me when we came to live in the cabin, and I named her after my cousin. Don't you know, Cousin Lottie died of scarlet fever soon after my father was killed. Those were hard days for a little girl!"

She read the letter, then sat with head bowed. "It all happened so long ago," she murmured. She picked up the bottle of glistening nuggets. "My father gave these to me for my birthday. He found them in the creek, stuck fast in crevices in the bedrock. See how rough they are? That told him that they'd come from someplace close by. When nuggets are washed a long way from the original ore body, the tumbling of the water and gravel wears them smooth. Later he did find the outcropping they'd come from, not far away in Morning Gulch."

"The gold you and your father hid—did it look like this?"

"No. That was crumbly quartz rock with bits and pieces of gold embedded in it. I remember he said that ore was special, because in that part of Washington, gold is usually so mixed with other minerals you can't see it."

"Did you ever find out if the gold ore you hid was as good as your father thought it would be?" Jodi questioned eagerly.

"No. My mother was so sad after the accident that she didn't want to go back. Then too, soon after that, the mining excitement died down. Even if the gold had proved out, don't you know, we couldn't have marketed it."

"Do you remember where you hid the ore?" Jodi asked. Mike poked her. Jodi knew he thought her rude, but she had to know.

Lucy Steincroft gave her breathless little laugh. "Yes. I remember that night well. We had a stable for the mules near the cabin, dug into the side of the hill. My father always made anything we did together into a game."

She paused, remembering. "That night we pretended we were pirates, hiding pieces of eight. I remember how Papa lit our kerosene lantern. He let me carry the bag of gold. We crept from tree to tree, with me holding on to his coattail."

"You hid it in the stable?"

"Yes. I can still see those mules rolling their eyes and crowding away from us. We must have been convincing pirates!"

"Would you care if we tried to find the stable?" Jodi asked eagerly.

"Not at all. And you are welcome to the ore if you

60

find it. But you will come back and tell me all about it, won't you?"

The cousins promised that they would. As they turned to go, Lucy called them back. She beckoned them close. "Look under the manger," she whispered. "Under a flat rock."

Mrs. Marsh was already home from work when they burst into the kitchen.

"Oh, Mom, sorry we're late, but wait until you hear what we've been doing!" Jodi caught her mother's hands and whirled her around.

"Goodness, daughter! It must have been exciting!"

Jodi described their meeting with Lucy. "You know, Mom," she said, "I was nervous about going to a place where everyone is old, but they seemed happy to see us. Miss Steincroft is so . . . so . . . real!"

Mrs. Marsh smiled. "Did you think she'd not be real?"

"Oh, Mom, you know what I mean." Jodi hurried on. "She told us where to find the gold that she and her father hid, and she said if we found it we could keep it. Mom, there just has to be a way we can spend more time at Morning Gulch."

"I wish there was. But I have to work, and you know how important your father's study time is to all of us. Besides, Will needs his truck every day, and we have no other way to travel. I don't know how we could do it."

A big lump rose in Jodi's throat. It just didn't seem fair.

Disaster
for Jodi

That night at dinner the cousins told their fathers about their afternoon with Lucy Steincroft.

"If only we could go back and look for the stable," sighed Jodi. "Just think, real hidden treasure!"

"I can't solve the problem of someone to go exploring with the kids," put in Uncle Will. "But I may have a solution to one of your problems, Alan."

All eyes turned to Billy's dad.

"Today I looked at a new Ford station wagon which had been in a bad smash-up. I put it on the rack. As far as I can tell, there's nothing wrong with the transmission. It could easily replace the one in your old wagon. Then if we found parts to rebuild your engine you'd have wheels again. What do you think?"

"Sounds great, Will. But you know I'm all thumbs when it comes to mechanical things. And we haven't funds right now to pay for the parts or your labor."

"We could get the transmission for almost nothing.

You could pay for the parts later. I wouldn't charge for the labor; I'd do it evenings, and the kids could help."

"Me too? Could I help too?" Jodi asked eagerly.

"You too, young lady, if you're not afraid of a little grease."

The next few evenings were spent with Uncle Will in the shop. Mike and Jodi didn't know a monkey wrench from a lug bolt, but Billy had helped his dad many times before.

With the wrecked car balanced overhead on the hoist, Jodi and Mike peered up into the mysterious underparts of the automobile. Billy tugged with a wrench, trying to loosen the bolts holding the transmission assembly. While he worked, he pointed out the different parts of the running gear and explained how each worked.

"I didn't know you knew so much about cars!"

Billy beamed at Mike's admiration. "My dad's a good teacher." He wiped his hands on his pants. "Dad, you want these small parts cleaned before we use them?"

Uncle Will had just freed the drive shaft. Billy and Mike sprang to help him lower it to the floor. "There's a big pan of solvent over there on the counter. Show them what to do, son."

Billy handed Jodi a grease-slathered gear cluster to clean. She held it away from her in distaste. "Ugh! Why does grease have to be so . . . greasy!"

She scrubbed away with a brush, trying to ignore the fumes of the solvent. Soon bare metal began to shine through. She worked out the last traces of dirty

63

grease and set the part to dry with the pieces Mike had cleaned.

The street outside the shop grew dark. "Nine o'clock," said Uncle Will. "Time to quit. We'd better wash up or Adele will never let us in the house."

Jodi looked down at her greasy hands and arms. Her jeans and T-shirt were greasy too. The mirror over the shop sink showed a black smear across her forehead and one on her nose.

"Now you know where the term 'grease monkey' comes from," teased her brother, looking over her shoulder into the mirror.

"You're every bit as grubby as I am, Michael Marsh! I hope we're really being some help. I don't like to get this dirty for nothing!"

By Wednesday Eliza had her new transmission. "Tonight we'll strip her down," Uncle Will planned. "I've been scouting through the junkers out back for parts. We'll need to buy only a few new parts to rebuild the engine."

"Uncle Will, could I clean the inside of the car while the rest of you work on the engine?"

"Sure, Jodi. Don't you like being a grease monkey?"

"Well, motors are interesting, but I'd rather work on the upholstery. I must have scrubbed my fingernails for half an hour last night and still didn't get them clean."

Mike hooted. "That's a girl for you!"

"Never mind, Mike," said his uncle. "She'll probably be busier than you tonight. Only so many people can work at this job at one time, anyway."

64

The next day after Billy's lessons, the boys rode their bikes to the shop to spend the day with Uncle Will. Jodi loaded the washer, then climbed the stairs to her room. Shelves lining one wall held her "museum," collections of pressed leaves and flowers, rocks, shells from the beach, bits of driftwood. And books, lots of them. She liked best to read of people who lived in bygone days. Maybe someday she'd be a history teacher like Dad. She picked up one of her books and curled up in the chair next to the window.

Beyond the neighboring roofs, the distant Cascades beckoned. Usually Jodi had only to open a book and she forgot everything going on around her. But today her thoughts kept straying to that lost mine up in those peaks, and Steincroft's hidden ore.

Just then the front door opened. Her mother called, "Anybody here?"

Jodi jumped from her chair and ran down the stairs. "Mom, why are you home so early?"

"I'm afraid I'm out of a job for a few days." Soot streaked Adele Marsh's white smock and her round, pleasant face. Her hair was disheveled. She went into the kitchen and got out the coffeepot. "A cup of coffee sounds good right now."

"Mom, tell me. What happened? Did you get fired?"

"Not the kind of 'fired' you're thinking about." Her mother laughed shakily. "One of the ovens shorted out, and the wall behind it caught fire. We put it out before the firemen arrived, but the whole building filled with smoke. The ovens are old, so the boss says he'll replace them while he's repairing the fire damage. He thought he'd be finished by Monday."

"Oh, Mom, I'm glad you're okay." Jodi hugged her mother. "What will you do with four whole days off?"

"There's always plenty to do."

The buzzer on the washer sounded. While Jodi put the first load into the drier and the next one into the washer, she heard her mother on the telephone.

"Listen to this, Jodi," she said, hanging up the receiver. "Will is driving the boys and their bikes home. I'll take him back to the shop and bring the pickup home with me. Dad stays late for class tonight anyway. He and Will won't mind batching for a couple of evenings. So you kids and I can drive up to the summer cabin this afternoon, and . . ."

"And we can look for the hidden ore! Super!" Jodi squealed.

They reached the valley around four o'clock that Thursday afternoon. Stopping only to make sure that everything was all right at the cabin, they drove on to the Morning Gulch trail.

Thunder jumped out of the back of the pickup as they stopped and scrambled into the brush with happy barking. Jodi and the boys hitched their packs to their shoulders. "Mom, sure you don't want to come along?"

"No thanks, dear. I'm going to enjoy some time all to myself at the cabin. Uncle Will plans to have Eliza running in time for him and Dad to drive up Saturday. You can show all of us Morning Gulch then."

"Okay, we'll see you sometime tomorrow," said Mike. "Wish us luck."

"I'll do better than that, right now. Let's take just a moment to talk to God before you go."

Mrs. Marsh held out her hands. The others linked

theirs with hers in a circle and bowed their heads. "Dear Lord," she prayed, "we know You're always with us, wherever we go. But we ask You to keep special watch over the kids on this hike. Keep them safe, and help them to have fun. In Jesus' name, Amen."

"Amen," they chorused. "'Bye."

They made good speed until they reached the slide area. Again they cut walking sticks.

"Know what?" panted Mike as they struggled upward through the brush. "If we come back here Saturday with the grown-ups, we should bring a machete and clear a trail through this slide."

"That's a good idea," Jodi answered. "I think Dad's got a machete in the storage shed at the cabin."

The air held a hint of evening damp by the time they rounded the clump of spruce in front of the old house.

"We made it!" Jodi took off her sailor's hat and ran her fingers through her curls. "What's the matter with Thunder, Billy?"

The big dog snuffled back and forth across the clearing, the hair on his shoulders standing on end. A growl rumbled in his throat as he nosed along the bottom of the cabin door.

"Don't know. Maybe some animal's been around. Here, boy!" He patted the dog's head. Thunder looked around uneasily.

"It'll be dark soon," said Mike. "We'd better get settled while we can still see." They pushed open the stubborn door and lugged their packs inside.

"We ought to sleep better than the last time, with

these air mattresses." Billy pulled his out and began to puff air into it.

Jodi wandered around the cabin, looking out the cobwebby window, lifting the stove lid, and looking into the cupboard. On top of the cupboard sat the saucers which they had used to hold the candle stubs. She picked one up. "This is odd. Did one of you boys knock this candle out of the hardened wax when we were here before?"

"Not me."

"Me either."

"And this chair is pulled away from the table. I'm sure I pushed all the chairs into place before we left."

"You're letting Thunder spook you into imagining things, Jodi." Mike busied himself with his air mattress.

Jodi bit back a retort and carried her pack up the stairs. But Mike's tone rankled. "Mr. Know-it-all," she muttered. "I distinctly remember putting each chair back where we found it, just before we went out the door." She laid out her sleeping bag and went back downstairs.

Billy unrolled his bag. "I'm all set. Anybody else as starved as I am?"

They ate their sandwiches sitting on boulders beside the stream. Jodi mixed cold drink powder with the icy creek water and added a purification tablet.

Mike eyed the tumbling stream. "I'd rather have a big drink of water, but Dad says we shouldn't drink from mountain streams unless we boil the water or use purification tablets.

68

Jodi made a face. "These tablets make plain water taste awful."

"The water looks perfectly clear to me," said Billy.

"Some streams have bacteria that can really make you sick," answered Mike. "Sometimes they come from careless people; sometimes from animals."

Billy changed the subject. "I saw some marshmallows when I got the sandwiches out. How about a campfire?"

"Sure! Why don't we carry some of these small pieces of driftwood to the cabin and have our fire there?" Jodi still couldn't shake the thought that someone else had been in the cabin. She would feel more secure where they could duck inside and shut the door.

Thunder stayed near, with none of his usual frisking about. After roasting the marshmallows, telling a few jokes and singing some campfire songs, they put out the fire and went to bed.

Next morning, Jodi looked out the back window as she pulled on her jeans and sweatshirt. Only a few muted birdcalls came up from the gully, although it was sunup, the time when birds usually sing loudest. A haze veiled the mountains.

Wood smoke drifted into the room. "Hey cook, rise and shine!" Mike yelled.

Jodi ran to the other window to look down at the boys building the campfire. "Flapjack mix is in the plastic bag," she called. "I'll cook them if you'll mix them."

She hurried down the stairs and grabbed the largest kettle from the cook kit. "Be right back. I'm going down to the creek and wash my face. I'll bring some water."

When she returned, Mike had a kettle and spoon in one hand, the bag of mix in the other. "You didn't put the recipe in. How'm I supposed to know how much to use?"

"Silly! Just put the mix in the kettle, then add water a little at a time until it looks like pancake batter."

"Oh." Mike did as she said. Meanwhile, Jodi dropped a smidgin of butter into the frypan heating over the fire. Mike handed her the batter. "It's a little lumpy but I guess it will do."

"Where's the pancake turner?" Jodi poured some batter into the sizzling butter, tilting the pan to spread it in a circle.

"Can't find it. Guess we didn't bring one."

"How am I supposed to turn the hotcakes?"

"You expected me to use *my* ingenuity," said Mike. "Let's see how good *yours* is."

"No problem," answered his sister. "I'll do it like the old-timers did it." She flipped the pan up, stopping with a jerk, at the same time giving a flick of the wrist. The cake rose from the pan, turned over and landed raw side down in the pan.

"Wow! Let me do the next one," begged Billy.

"All right, but you eat every one you drop!"

Billy's first cake landed in the ashes. He flipped it out with a stick and called Thunder to eat it.

"No fair, Billy!"

"I'll do it right this time. Watch."

The next cake landed half in, half out of the pan. He scraped it onto his plate with his fork after a few minutes, and poured syrup over the rumpled heap. "How about cooking me a few while I eat this one, Jodi?"

When the batter was gone, Jodi rinsed the dishes in the creek. The boys rolled the beds and deflated air mattresses. Jodi carried water back to sprinkle over the embers of the campfire, stirring the ashes with a stick to be sure no spark remained.

Billy came out to watch her. His red thatch stuck up in all directions. No one had remembered to bring a comb and she knew her hair must look just as bad. Billy pushed his glasses up and said briskly, "Where do we start?"

"Start?"

"To look for the stable."

Jodi gazed at the forest around them. Mossy ridges marked the remains of trees that had fallen years before. Windfalls hung in the branches of other trees or lay like barriers on the forest floor. Brush grew thick where enough light reached the ground. She could see nothing that looked like the stable Lucy Steincroft had described.

Mike came out of the cabin in time to hear Billy's question.

"Boy, if we aren't smart!" he said disgustedly. "We should have asked Miss Steincroft where it was. All we know is that it was dug into the hillside somewhere near the cabin."

"There's a lot of hillside here. We'd better get going." Jodi started off into the brush.

"Take it easy, Jodi! Let's approach this scientifically." Mike waited for her to return. "Remember, that all happened more than seventy years ago. There may even be trees growing over the place."

"Sounds like a waste of energy to even try to find it," said Billy. He plopped down on the ground and leaned back on Thunder, who was napping by the cabin door.

"If it's here, we'll find it. Come on over to the edge of the gully."

Mike beckoned Billy to a spot about twenty feet from the cabin. "Jodi, you stand here." He positioned her five feet from Billy, and placed himself an equal distance beyond Jodi. "Now, what we do is walk in a semicircle around the cabin until we reach the edge of the gully on the far side of it. Then we'll just move over and start back the other way, making bigger semicircles every time."

"Oh, I get it. That way we won't miss anything."

The first set of semicircles went easily, but as they moved farther out, the going got rougher. Thickets of trees, heavy moss, the dips and humps of the forest floor, could easily conceal any sign of fallen timbers. The stable might be anywhere.

After struggling through the woods for what seemed ages, Jodi sat down to rest. She felt hot and sweaty. Scratches stung where branches had grabbed her bare arms. She leaned against a tree trunk.

"Finding that stable is impossible," she thought. "It just isn't here anymore . . . if it ever was. Maybe Lucy just imagined that part of the story." She squinted through the branches above. The sky was definitely overcast now. The air felt muggy.

Several feet away, something caught her eye.

Sticking out of the trunk of a sizable spruce tree and higher than a tall man could reach was a long, four-sided metal spike. Its uneven surface told her it had been hand forged.

A cascade of hardened pitch poured to the ground from the spot where the spike pierced the tree. Some of it looked white and crystallized, but colors of purple, green, black, and amber showed through. Some was new enough to be sticky. Jodi guessed that the growth of the tree had carried the spike much higher than it was when first hammered into the trunk. As the tree grew, the wound continued to open and bleed.

She thought of calling the boys to come and look, but decided she'd better not let them know she'd taken time out. She heard them shouting to each other further along the hillside.

Jodi got up to scramble around the tree where she'd rested. The hillside here was steep; beyond the tree was a short but almost vertical drop. She would try to work her way along above it.

Suddenly she gave a wild yell.

Mike crashed through the brush toward the yell, Billy behind him. Jodi was nowhere to be seen.

Then a muffled wail floated up through the floor of the forest. "Hel-l-lp! Mike! Hel-l-lp!"

More Discoveries

"Jodi! Where are you?" Mike yelled.

"I don't know, but I want out. Hel-l-lp!"

The panicky voice seemed to come from under his feet. Moving cautiously forward, Mike and Billy saw a hole in the hillside just above the drop-off Jodi had tried to avoid. Mike reached for the flashlight hanging at his belt. He clung to overhanging branches and shined his light into the hole.

Jodi's scared and dirty face looked up at him.

"She's done it, Billy! You've done it, Jodi! You found the stable!"

"I don't care what I found. I want out!"

"We'll get you out. Are you hurt?"

"I don't think so. But Mike, get me out of here. I can't breathe in a place like this!"

"Catch." Mike tossed Jodi the flashlight. "We're moving back so we won't fall in too. Just give us time to think of something."

Jodi flashed the light around her prison. The front

wall of the dugout had fallen outward long ago, allowing the front ends of the roof logs to drop too. Only a narrow, triangular space remained between the slanting logs and back wall.

Jodi fought a suffocating fear that rose in her chest. "Oh, God, the space is so small. Help me be calm."

From somewhere came the thought, "When I am afraid . . ." Where had she heard that before? Oh, yes. Sunday school class last week. She'd looked up the verse herself and read it to the class. "When I am afraid, I will trust in You."

"Lord, I do trust You," she prayed. "But help them hurry." She found herself gazing at a heap of poles at her feet, so rotted they were almost one mass of decaying wood. They crumbled when she pushed at them.

"Why, that must have been the manger," she whispered.

She heard Billy's voice above. "You know, those logs are so rotten the rest of them could collapse anytime. We'd better try to get her out of there right away and forget about the ore."

"I think so too. Jodi?"

"Yes, Mike?"

"Don't move. I'm going back to the cabin for a hatchet."

"You kidding? There's no place to move to!"

"What can I do?" Billy called after Mike.

"Just stay there so we don't lose her again!"

Trying to ignore the bits of dirt still dribbling down on her, Jodi carefully pushed aside the rotten poles of the manger to make more room. Underneath were several large flat rocks, laid close together to form a sort of paving.

"To keep the mule's feed off the dirt floor?" she wondered. "Lucy said they buried the ore under a flat rock, beneath the manger."

She tried to lift the nearest rock with her fingertips. It was firmly embedded in the dirt. A couple of chunks of rotted wood fell from above. She smothered a shriek.

Setting the flashlight down, Jodi pried at the stubborn rock. It didn't move. She dug at the others, with no luck. Shoving away more debris, she felt a rock move slightly. With a grunt, she lifted it, and in the hollow left in the dirt floor, something glittered. For a moment she forgot where she was as she gazed astonished at a heap of whitish quartz chunks, richly streaked with shining gold. The bag that once held them had rotted away in the dampness, leaving the ore unharmed.

Jodi searched in her pockets for something to carry it in. Nothing. Glancing around the narrow space, she saw a glimmer of white in the flashlight's beam. Her sailor's cap! She pulled it from beneath a chunk of wood and brushed off the dirt.

Then she squatted and carefully scooped the glistening heap into her cap with her hands. Almost forgetting her fear, she shivered with excitement. What if they could find the mine from which this had come? What couldn't they do with a whole mine full of this fabulous stuff?

Hearing voices above, Jodi got to her feet, careful not to spill the ore.

"Stand back, Jodi. Here comes your ladder!"

A shower of dirt fell as the butt end of a small alder came sliding into the hole. Jodi reached out to guide the makeshift ladder to the floor. Mike had trimmed the top and branches from the tree, leaving stubs of branches three to four inches long.

"Come on up, but be careful!"

Like a squirrel, Jodi scrambled up the ladder. As her head and shoulders poked through the hole, the ladder slid sideways against the roof logs. The logs began to sink under her.

"Quick!" Mike grabbed her outstretched hand and pulled. More of the roof collapsed under her scrambling feet as Mike pulled her to safety.

"Whew! I was never so glad to get out of a place," she panted.

"Boy, Jodi," Billy shook his head. "When you set out to find something, you really put your whole self into it, don't you?"

"Funny, funny! Anyway, Billy, my method worked. Look here!"

She held out her cap. "Yipee!" whooped Billy. "We're rich! We're rich!"

"Take it easy!" grinned Mike. "We're not rich. Not unless we find the mine this came from. And maybe not even then."

"Rich or not, how many kids find real buried treasure?" Jodi folded the brim of her cap over the precious cargo. "After all that I'm absolutely parched."

"Me too. *And* hungry," chimed Billy.

The creek ran past only fifty feet from the stable. Not even thinking about possible bacteria, Jodi knelt to gulp the sweet water from her cupped hands. She splashed it over her face and arms to wash away the dirt and bits of rotten wood. Then she flung out her arms as if to embrace the whole wide out-of-doors. Free!

Back at the cabin they ate the sandwiches remaining from last night. Then they put their packs together, preparing to leave. As they finished, the sun broke through the overcast. Jodi walked to the gully behind the cabin and looked across. "I've got an idea, you guys."

"Let's hear it."

"Why don't we follow the opposite edge of the gully above the rock wall over there, 'til it runs into the ridge. If we follow the ridge down, we should run right into the trail. There'll be a good view of the cabin area from up there."

"Aw, let's not. Getting through that brush down there wouldn't be any picnic."

"I didn't mean to go *through* the gully, Billy. If we follow the creek we could cross the mouth of the gully and climb up where the hillside comes down to the creek."

"We've got what we came after—and don't you think you've been in enough trouble for one day, Jodi?" Mike sounded like a big brother again.

But Jodi held her tongue. She'd try another tactic. "If we went that way we could see if anyone has prospected over there," she said.

"It might be a good place to look for exposed ore veins at that," said Mike. "And it probably won't take more than an hour longer. Okay, I'll go along with your idea, Jodi. You want to follow the trail and wait for us up on the ridge, Billy?"

78

Billy thought it over. "No. I'll go with you. I don't want to meet a bear or something all by myself."

Mike laughed. "You'd make a pretty tasty meal for a 'bear or something.' Let's go, everybody!"

They followed the stream until they came to a small creek running out of the gully to join the large one. They hopped across on stones and began the climb.

They passed through a stand of gnarled big-leaf maples. Glossy licorice fern sprouted from crevices in the mossy trunks. Jodi reached up to pull a fern loose. She scraped the bark off the long root and handed a piece to Billy.

"Taste this," she said. "See why it's called licorice fern?"

Billy chewed a moment, then spat. "Yeah, I see. Never did like licorice."

"Let's get higher," suggested Mike. They scrambled upward over the jumble of boulders, fallen trees, and brush.

"Isn't this a trail?" called Billy, who was somewhat higher than the others.

"Deer trail," said Mike.

He and Jodi followed Billy along the winding trail, skirting boulders and logs, until it stopped against a big rock outcrop. Below the rock, the ground fell away in a steep slope.

"What now?" asked Billy. "We can't climb that."

"Go left around it."

Working his way around the outcropping, Billy stopped suddenly. Jodi, close behind, stumbled against him. "Hey," he exclaimed, "Somebody did prospect over here!"

79

"Is it a real mine?"

"Don't think so," said Mike. "These are the tailings—the rock from the mine—that we're standing on here. You can tell they didn't take much out."

Jodi crept to the cavelike opening. The blackness inside seemed absolute. "O-o-h, it's spooky!" Her voice echoed eerily from the rocky walls. Inside, water dripped. She tossed a stone. It made a rain-barrel echo as it fell onto the damp floor.

Mike dropped his pack. "Here, let's use the flashlight. We'll only go a little way." The excavation was narrow; narrow enough to touch both sides with outstretched hands.

Thunder sat at the entrance, whining uneasily. Jodi wished she could stay with him, but she made herself follow the others. She stifled a yell as a big drop of water splashed against her forehead. Mud squished beneath her feet.

"Well, this is it!" said Mike after they had gone about thirty feet. His light flickered over a solid rock wall.

Jodi gratefully followed the boys toward the daylight at the other end of the tunnel. Near the entrance, her eyes fell on the footprints they'd left in the mud on their way in. Something about one of the marks didn't seem right.

"Give me the light, Mike."

"What did you find?"

"This heelprint—there's something odd about it."

"Looks just like the print my boot heels make," said Mike.

"But I caught a glimpse of it past you, before you

got to this spot on your way out. And it's going toward the entrance. You didn't turn around and look back, did you, on your way in?"

"Might have. What's wrong with you, Jodi? Never saw you so easily spooked before!"

Jodi ignored his remark. She flashed the light over the other footprints they had made in the mud. "But can't you see the difference? Ours look wet inside. This one is sort of dried out and not so sharp."

The boys bent over to look. Mike set his foot in the dirt beside the heelprint and stepped down. He squatted to inspect the two prints. "Not quite the same size, are they? Let's see your boots, Billy. Jodi?"

"Ours both have a waffly pattern on the bottoms," observed Billy.

"Someone *has* been snooping around." Jodi felt the hair on the back of her neck prickle.

"Come on, Sis! That footprint's probably been there for years." But the note of uncertainty in Mike's voice belied the confidence of his words, and the three cousins resumed their climb in silence.

Soon Jodi saw the afternoon sunlight glinting off the bright granite rock through the trees ahead of them. Mike angled more steeply upward so that they would come out above the rocks. Soon they broke out of the evergreens onto the bare rock at the edge of the bluff. A few trees clung here and there to ledges on the cliff. They could look down through their tops across the gully to the Steincroft cabin.

"It looks like a toy from up here," Jodi murmured.

"The first miners came from those mountains to the east," Mike told Billy. "Remember, we said that one

81

of the first routes to the mining areas on this side of the Cascades went through Morning Gulch?"

They moved ahead, now through trees, now scrambling over the rock near the edge of the bluff. Thunder raced on up the mountainside. From time to time they heard him yip as he followed animal trails in the woods above.

Suddenly they found themselves on a ledge, the bluff rising on one side and a vertical drop on the other.

"What do we do, go back all that way?" Billy's shoulders slumped.

"Sure looks like it. And we're so close to the ridge!" Jodi felt discouraged too.

"I think we can make it." Mike walked to where the ledge narrowed and dropped away. "These rocks are steep, but looks like we can find footholds all the way across. Just don't look down!"

Mike slid over a boulder to a ledge below it. From there he picked his way out onto the rockface, clinging with his hands as he felt his way with his feet. The others followed, stopping where the ledge widened a little. They waited while Mike peered ahead.

"Not far now, guys. But watch every step." He began to work his way around an overhanging chunk of rock. Billy started to follow. Jodi suddenly felt as though her heart had gone plummeting down an elevator shaft. One moment her cousin's shoulder was next to hers, the next, she saw only his hands scrabbling desperately at the edge of the rock where she stood.

Lucy's Warning

"Help us, Mike!" Jodi screamed.

Without thinking, she flung herself to the narrow ledge and grabbed Billy's wrists. In a moment Mike knelt beside her. Together they pulled with all their strength, until Billy sat gasping on the ledge. "Th-thanks! If my feet hadn't hit a bump in that rock, I'd have had it!"

Mike was shaking. "I told you not to look down!" he blurted angrily.

"I didn't. Scout's honor!"

"Then what happened?" asked Jodi.

The color began to come back behind Billy's freckles. "I'm not sure. I'd just stepped out to follow Mike, and something—a bright flash—hit me in the eyes. At the same time a loose rock rolled under my foot . . ."

"Must have been the sun."

"No. The flash came from those trees down there, directly across from us."

"Nothing there now."

"Yes, there is, Mike," Jodi said quickly. "I just saw something move in the trees."

"*I* don't see a thing." Mike began again to work his way around the rock. "I was crazy to agree to taking this route. This time, watch what you're doing." Mike's words were gruff, but Jodi knew it was only because he'd had such a scare. Billy might have been badly hurt. Even killed.

Before long they reached the ridgetop trail over which they'd come to the cabin. Billy whistled for Thunder. Two hours later they were hiking down the logging road toward the summer cottage and dinner.

The cousins slept late on Saturday morning. Mrs. Marsh drove to the nearby ranger station to telephone her husband while the three ate breakfast. The ore glittered in a glass jar on the table.

"Hope our dads get here early," Jodi said between bites of cereal. "Can't wait to show them where we found the ore, and the cabin—and the gulch."

Mike had been scornful of Jodi's feeling that someone was snooping around their discoveries at Morning Gulch. This morning she could easily believe that her imagination might have played tricks. So she didn't speak of her suspicions again, nor did anyone bring up Billy's close call on the rockface.

"But I know You were with us, Lord," she prayed silently. "And I do thank You for watching over us."

At that moment Mrs. Marsh returned. "Well, kids, looks like your fathers can't make it after all. One of the profs gave Dad some extra research to do before Monday, and Will hasn't found time to work on Eliza yet."

"Oh, shoot! Would you like to hike up to the gulch anyway, even if they can't go along, Mom?"

"Thanks, Jodi, but I'll wait for the men. There'll be another chance."

"Let's try some fishing then," suggested Mike.

The boys and Thunder went off along the river

bank, while Jodi settled down in the hammock with a book. A couple of hours later the boys returned.

"Any luck?" Jodi asked.

"You bet!" Billy's ruddy face glowed with pride. "Just look at this." He opened the creel. It was half full of rainbow trout, their sides still shimmering with the pink and green iridescence that gave them their name. He held up a fourteen-inch beauty. "And I caught the biggest one!"

"If we hurry, we could get home by suppertime and surprise our men with a fish fry," said Mrs. Marsh. "What do you say, kids?"

"Great! On the backyard barbecue, Mom?"

"I don't see why not."

That evening, around the picnic table, everyone dug into platefuls of potato salad and crusty trout.

"Delicious!" Uncle Will pronounced. "I'd say your trip was a real success."

"Oh, but wait 'til you see what else we brought home." Jodi ran into the house and came back with the jar of ore. She unscrewed the lid and spilled some of it into her father's hand. Then she described how she'd found it, and how the boys had rescued her.

"You really threw yourself into that project, Jodi!" Her father laughed.

"That's just what I told her," said Billy.

Alan Marsh's face grew sober. "Seriously though, the consequences of that tumble could have been much worse. You must be extremely cautious anytime you're in the woods alone."

"We *did* try to be careful, Dad." Jodi remembered

Billy's two close calls: in the stream, and on the bluff behind the cabin. Was it wrong not to tell Mom and Dad? After all, she and Mike couldn't have prevented either of the incidents. Or could they? Yesterday, for instance. They did take chances in crossing that rockface.

Monday the three cousins paid another visit to the Mountain View Nursing Home. Pleasant Mrs. Kratz met them. This time she asked them to wait in the lobby.

"Miss Steincroft enjoys sitting up for short periods. And you'll have some privacy out here."

Soon she came back, pushing Lucy in a wheelchair. The little lady wore a soft knitted shawl, blue as a robin's egg. An afghan was tucked over her lap.

She beamed at the young people. Taking both Jodi's hands in hers she chuckled, "When Mrs. Kratz told me I had visitors, I knew it would be you. You found the stable, didn't you? Was the gold where I said it would be?"

Jodi grinned back at her. "It was exactly where you said it would be." She took the jar from her bookbag and opened it for Lucy to see.

"Ah, yes. Beautiful! But where is the leather bag?"

"Well, you see, Miss Steincroft, you hid it a long time ago . . ."

"Of course. It had rotted away. But tell me—tell me all about your adventure."

So the three told her everything, even Jodi's suspicions that someone had been spying. She listened to this soberly. "I never went back to Morning Gulch, but I know this country well. I taught in the mountain towns for years. There used to be prospectors up in those hills, hoping to make a last big strike. There are probably still a few left."

She paused to catch her breath. "Most are harmless enough, but living alone the way they do, forty, fifty years, some are bound to be a little strange. And there are other dangers too. My nephew says that nowadays there are even marijuana growers hiding out in the woods. You shouldn't be up in that country with no grown-up along, don't you know?"

"We can take care of ourselves, Miss Steincroft." Even to himself, Mike's words must have sounded brash. Lucy gave him a sharp look through her little gold-rimmed spectacles. He squirmed.

"Nevertheless, if you think someone is watching you, promise you'll take one of your parents along if you go back." The old lady seemed so concerned that Jodi and Billy said together, "We promise," and Mike added, "Okay."

Lucy returned the jar to Jodi. "You children keep this. When you look at it you can think, 'Somewhere in Morning Gulch there is a mine full of who knows how much ore, just like this.'"

Jodi bounced on the edge of the sofa where she and the boys sat together. "Oh, I wish we could find the mine!"

"Me too," blurted Billy. "Can we . . . I mean, do you mind . . . if we look for the mine?"

"No, of course I don't mind. The claim has gone back to the government. Anyone is free to look, don't you know?" She paused. "Did I tell you that some years after we left our claim, two of my father's employees went back to try to open the mine? They cleared out some of the tunnel. They found my father's remains under the rubble, but they ran out of money before they succeeded in reopening the mine."

Mike had listened thoughtfully. "Miss Steincroft, where should we look?"

"Look? Let me see. I remember climbing a long time to reach the mine. I thought at the time we must be at the very top of the mountain. And seems to me it faced east—yes, toward the sunrise. That's why it was called the Morning Mine. I remember—there was a building below it where my father's helpers stayed."

Just then the nurse left the desk where she had been writing and crossed to the wheelchair. "Miss Steincroft, we don't want to tire you. How are you feeling?"

"I'm fine, young woman. Don't go treating me like some old fogy!" But she patted the nurse's hand affectionately.

"Let me know when you're through visiting." Mrs. Kratz returned to her desk.

Lucy reached under the afghan and drew out three small tissue-wrapped packages. She handed one to each of the cousins. "I wanted you to have something special to remember me by. I hope you like them."

Jodi tore the paper from hers. "Oh, it's beautiful!" she exclaimed. She held up a filigreed pin, centered with a cluster of nuggets. Each of the boys unwrapped a tie tack made of bits of gold. "They were made from the gold in your treasure bag, weren't they, Miss Steincroft?"

"Yes. They're to thank you for the way you've brightened these past few weeks for me. And Jodi, you are just the person I'd like to have take care of my Lottie."

She handed Jodi the little wooden doll. To Jodi's embarrassment, she felt a tear roll down her cheek. She brushed it away and found her voice. "Oh, Miss Steincroft, thank you. I will take care of her. And every time I see her, I'll think of you." Impulsively she flung her arms around the old lady's neck and kissed her soft cheek.

"Bless you, child. And you too, boys. Come again soon."

Mrs. Kratz appeared to wheel Lucy back to her bed.

Jodi broke the silence on the bus ride home. "Isn't Miss Steincroft the dearest person? I wish there was something really nice we could do for her."

"I think we've already done it, whether we realized it or not," Mike answered.

"What's that?"

"Just being her friends."

"Oh. But I meant something we could *do*."

"Know what I wish?" interjected Billy. "I wish we could find that mine."

"Now that we know where to look, we just might find it. We just might!" Jodi wondered why she had ever feared that the summer might be dull.

The
Search

That night both families got together to roast marshmallows in the backyard fireplace. Afterwards they lounged on the grass, watching the first stars come out.

Suddenly Jodi sat up. "Listen, everybody. We showed you the gifts Miss Steincroft gave us, but we forgot the rest of it. She told us where the mine is located!"

"Not exactly, Jodi," said Mike. "She told us what she remembered. That might not be the same thing."

"Well . . . you're right." Jodi turned to the three adults. "But she remembered pretty clearly. Wouldn't it be exciting to look for the mine?"

Alan Marsh smiled. "You're very convincing, Jodi. Tell you what. Thursday is the Fourth of July . . ."

"A four-day weekend!" interrupted Billy. "Hey, Dad, do you get Thursday and Friday off?"

"I own my own business, remember? I can *take* them off."

"What about you, Mom?" asked Jodi.

"The bakery will be closed on the Fourth, but I'm afraid I'll have to work Friday, the next day."

Jodi's face fell. "Oh, Mom!"

"Now wait a minute. That doesn't have to affect the rest of you. Alan, if you can spare the time, you and Will take the kids and go to Morning Gulch. A few days away will do you both good."

"You wouldn't mind, Mom? Really?" Jodi leaped to her feet. "Yippee!"

Tuesday and Wednesday passed quickly. Mornings Jodi tutored Billy. The boys spent afternoons at the shop, working on old Eliza under Uncle Will's supervision. Jodi baked cookies for the trip, and biked to the camper's supply store to buy dehydrated food. Wednesday evening the boys and Uncle Will drove the station wagon home.

"Here you are, Adele!" said her brother. "You'll have your own wheels this weekend. You can go to Morning Gulch with us, and drive back to town Friday morning. What do you think of that?"

"What would we have done without you, Will? Eliza's running again, with almost no cost to us, when we thought she was ready for the junkyard!"

"The engine still needs a tune-up. I'll take my tools along and try to get that miss out of there before you return to town."

Thursday morning the boys and Thunder squeezed into the pickup's cab beside Uncle Will, while Jodi rode with her parents in the old green Ford. All went well until the road began to wind up into the mountains.

Then the protesting noises from under the hood became so insistent that Mr. Marsh pulled over beside the road.

Will Skarson stopped the pickup behind them.

"Trouble?"

Jodi's dad told him of the noises.

"Better not drive it 'til I can take a look at it. There's a chain in the pickup. Let me give you a tow to the cabin."

Alan Marsh caught a glimpse of Jodi's face in the rearview mirror. "Why the gloom, daughter?"

"I suppose this means you grown-ups will spend the day fixing Eliza, and we won't get to look for the mine."

"I'm sorry, Jodi, but Mom has to have a way to get back to town tomorrow."

"Now, Alan. Why can't I drive the pickup back while you and Will fix our car later this weekend? This doesn't have to spoil our plans."

Jodi brightened again. They left the station wagon at the cabin. Everyone piled into the pickup for the ride to the trail.

When they came to the old slide area, the boys went first with the machetes, hacking a trail through the brush. The others hurled the branches out of the path as they came along behind.

"How did you ever get through this before? Even with a path cleared, it's still hard going."

"Wasn't easy, Mom." Jodi lifted a branch of devil's club with her stick and tossed it out of the way.

They were all glad to reach the shade of the big trees at the upper edge of the slide. "There's our pickup!" Uncle Will pointed to the road winding through the trees far below.

His sister wiped her face with a bandanna. "That's a long, hot walk, but isn't it a gorgeous day? Perfect July weather!"

When they reached the creek, everyone stopped again. Jodi beckoned to Billy. "I thought I'd run on ahead to be sure the cabin's okay. Want to come?"

Rounding the clump of hemlocks, Jodi and Bill saw Thunder waiting in the sunlight in front of the cabin. His tail wagged happily.

"Thunder doesn't act like anything's wrong this time," said Billy.

They walked over to the little house and pushed open the door. "Everything's fine in here, too," she said.

Just then Mike stepped into the clearing, the adults right behind. Jodi sprang to the door and bowed low. "Welcome to the 'Wilderness Hilton,'" she called.

"So this is the famous Steincroft cabin!" Mr. Marsh looked it over appraisingly. "It really is in pretty good shape for its age, isn't it?"

"Come in and look around," Jodi said eagerly. "Come on, Mom. I want you to see Lucy's room."

The adults followed her up the creaking stairs, Thunder squeezing around legs to be first into the loft. Jodi opened the shutters to let the light stream in.

"See, here's her bed, and the little table and chair." They admired the sturdy home-built furniture and looked out over the gully behind the cabin. "And look." Jodi put her hand into the crevice between rafter and ceiling. "Here's where I found her treasure bag."

Downstairs, the men leafed through the stack of

old magazines while Jodi and her mother stored the food supplies inside the cupboard.

"I hope we brought enough groceries," Billy commented. "Isn't it lunchtime yet?"

Mrs. Marsh hugged her nephew. "Lunch coming right up. Want to eat here?"

"Let's go down to the creek," Jodi suggested. "It's nice and cool there. Then we can show you the stable, and then go up to the gulch."

Smooth boulders made seats, and the gurgle of the stream, background music for a pleasant lunch.

Jodi threw the last scrap of her sandwich to Thunder. She hopped from her rock. "Come on, let's go see the stable."

"Can't the rest of us finish our lunch, Miss Impatience?" Her father laughed.

"Sorry. Maybe I'll have another sandwich myself."

But soon they were all picking their way over the forested slope. Jodi glimpsed the big spruce with the spike in its trunk ahead of them. "Careful now. There's what's left of the stable." She pointed toward the hole through which she had fallen, the end of Mike's makeshift ladder still sticking out.

Her mother gasped. "Jodi! You could have been hurt!"

Dad poked at the broken logs exposed when Jodi tumbled into the stable. "Now, Adele. She *wasn't* hurt. Who would have suspected there was ever a building here at all?"

Jodi flashed her dad a grateful look.

The grown-ups marveled at the spruce, with its cascade of hardened pitch glinting in the sunlight filtering through the branches. "Probably Steincroft put that spike there to hang his lantern on while he fed his mules," Alan Marsh commented. The woods were still, except for the rushing of the creek and a squirrel scolding in the distance.

Mike broke into their thoughts. "Everybody ready for a hike up the gulch?"

"Lead on," his father answered.

Mike led the way across the foot log over the creek. A short walk upward through the timber brought them to the bottom of the gulch.

"Here's the prospect hole," said Jodi as they continued up the gulch and came round the big boulders in front of the shaft. "We thought we'd found the lost mine when we saw this hole."

Uncle Will found the stalactites, little icicles of minerals left behind by dripping water, especially interesting. "I always thought these took thousands of years to form. Look, this one's several inches long already."

The one he examined broke off in his hand. He brought it out in the sunlight where Jodi waited.

"Could I have it if you don't want it, Uncle Will? I'll put it in my museum." He gave it to her and she put the stone icicle in her pocket.

"Now, where should we look first for the Morning Mine?" she asked.

"Lucy told us it was near the top of the gulch and it faced the sunrise," said Mike. "So it's up there somewhere, across from where we are now." He waved his hand in a wide arc.

"Those weren't very specific directions when you

see all that territory up there." Mrs. Marsh gazed at the steep slope rising opposite and sweeping on toward the top of the pass. The slope was broken by rocky promontories. Thickets of vine maple, bushes, and stunted evergreens clung here and there.

"I think the best plan is to hike all the way to the top of the pass. If we haven't spotted it by then, we can search on the way down," suggested Mr. Marsh.

They clambered upward. "Whew! It's getting hotter!" panted Billy. "I'm getting tired."

"Me too. But we're almost to the top." Jodi stopped to scan the cliffs.

"No mine up there," said Mike.

"It's got to be there," asserted Jodi. "Don't give up yet."

Some time later the group straggled to the top of the pass. They looked down the other side. The spot where they stood formed part of the rim of a bowl-shaped hollow. Below them a cliff dropped several hundred feet to a round blue lake in the bottom of the bowl. A small glacier calved chunks of ice into the lake. Beyond, valleys and ridges and peaks stretched as far as the eye could see.

Jodi looked at the blue jewel below. "That looks like one of those lakes the glaciers carved—what do you call it, Dad?"

"Glacial cirque? That's what it is, all right. The first miners came through those mountains to the southeast and through this pass where we're standing now."

Jodi turned to look back the way they had come. The promontories on the side of Morning Gulch cast a multitude of shadows in the clear mountain light. Any of them could hide the entrance to the mine. "I wish we'd brought binoculars," she said.

"The tunnel might be completely blocked, or overgrown with brush," Alan Marsh said. "Looks like we'll have to spread out and work our way along the wall as best we can."

"Why don't we go in partners?" suggested Jodi.

She found herself paired for the search with Billy. Thunder made three, but he wasn't much help. They followed the swoop of the pass to where it merged with the top of the east-facing wall. The others moved along the side of the gulch, climbing up to investigate any promising cleft or cave.

The cousins found the going easy at first. But as the distance to the floor of the gulch increased, the wall itself became more vertical. Finally they scrambled across a rocky buttress to find that part of the wall ahead became a sheer cliff.

"We'd better climb down here," said Jodi. "If we go farther we might not be able to *get* down."

Billy whistled to Thunder, who followed them over the rock outcropping. He pushed past, sending stones bouncing down the slope to a level, grassy ledge.

A pocket-sized pika, like a little guinea pig, watched, motionless, as the dog skidded down the slope. Now in a flash it disappeared behind a rock. Thunder glimpsed the movement. With a shrill bark he leaped after it.

Jodi heard gravel rolling, and Thunder's yips floating back.

The ledge where Thunder had spied the pika led around the rib of rock. They followed as it dipped into a hollow. Another bulge of rock lay ahead. The first pika had scurried to safety, but Thunder discovered another on the next outcropping. It too disappeared, but Thunder charged after it, up and over the rocks. They heard his high-pitched bark of excitement.

"Sounds like he's got it cornered," said Billy. "Shall we go see?"

They ran through the hollow and clambered over the rocks to find Thunder just over the crest of the outcropping. He thrust his nose into a crevice under a boulder. His long tail swept the air in time with his burst of barking.

Billy flopped down beside him to look under the rock and laughed. "It's hopeless, old fellow! You can't dig through solid rock!"

Jodi raised her eyes to the cliff above them. The outcropping sloped into the wall of the gulch, widening out to form a sort of platform just ahead, overlooking the valley. Just past them a shadowed cleft split the wall. A bulge of rock hid the lower part of the fissure.

Billy sat up. "Where are you going, Jodi?"

"Just want to see what's behind . . ." Jodi froze in mid-stride. Slowly she lowered her foot. Without turning, she motioned to her cousin, and squeaked, "Billy, come here, quick!"

A Ghost
from the Past

Jodi took a deep breath and tried again. "Billy, come quick! It's the mine!"

Just beyond the bulge of rock a narrow black slot pierced the face of the cliff. Awestruck, she whispered to Billy, "This has to be it. It's near the top of the mountain, and it faces east."

"Wow!"

"It's bigger than the other holes we found," she said. "And look at all the timbers."

Heavy wooden beams framed the opening. Two rusty iron rails ran back into the tunnel.

"Let's call the others!" Billy hurried to where he could look out over the gulch. Jodi followed in a daze. If only Lucy could be with them now!

As they stood looking down into Morning Gulch, Jodi realized that the broken rock filling the cleft below and in front of them had been taken from inside the mine itself. A scatter of great boulders along the bottom of the wall helped conceal the broken rock from people below.

"Look, Billy!" Jodi pointed to the base of the tailings pile. A few yards beyond lay a pile of gray and broken boards, all that was left of the miner's shack Lucy had mentioned.

At first they could see none of the other searchers. Then they saw Jodi's parents. They shouted at the top of their lungs. The two little figures turned to stare up at the wall, then signaled to Mike and Uncle Will, who were out of sight from where Billy and Jodi stood. The cousins slid down the tailings pile and ran to meet them.

Soon all of them clustered around the mine entrance. Suitably impressed, Mrs. Marsh said, "Do you realize that we may be the first people to stand here since the mine was abandoned?"

Billy patted his dog. "We'd never have found it without Thunder."

Jodi's father poked at the nearest timber with his pocket knife.

"What are you doing, Dad?"

"These braces are pretty rotten," he answered. "If they're all like this we'll have to stay out. Let me borrow your flashlight, Mike." Its beam played over more heavy timbers supporting the walls and roof of the tunnel. Stepping inside, he cut into several of the braces. "These are soft outside, but firm underneath. Come on in, but watch your step."

The light flickering over the tunnel walls cast eerie shadows on the faces of the little group. Jodi held her father's sleeve as the others crowded close behind. The familiar sensation of panic welled up inside her even with all the others near. Here and there rivulets of water dripped down the walls. The air felt cold and dank.

"Ho! What have we here?" Dad flashed the light over a highsided metal cart, rusty as the rails beneath it.

Mike bent to examine one end of the cart. "Looks like this was made to connect with something else, Dad."

"It was. Miners fastened several of these ore carts together in a string and pulled them out to the tailings pile with a horse."

Billy gave the cart a shove. It didn't move. He put his shoulder against it and shoved again. This time it creaked ahead a few inches.

The tunnel curved gradually to the right as they moved along. Jodi turned to look back, just as the sliver of daylight marking the mine entrance blinked out. At the same time she struck her toe sharply against a rock on the floor. She yelped and clutched her father's arm tighter.

"Come on, Sis," Mike snorted. "Some treasure hunter you make!"

Jodi felt her face grow hot. She took a deep breath and clamped her mouth shut. "Nothing's going to make me holler again," she vowed silently. Dad flashed the light over the floor ahead.

"More rocks. Did they fall from the ceiling? No, looks solid there."

They moved along cautiously. The light fell against more fragments filling the tunnel ahead with a barrier of broken rock.

Something winked from the litter of rock spreading

toward them. Jodi pried out a crumpled metal object, heavy for its size and badly discolored. "What do you suppose this was?"

Her dad took the object and looked at it closely. "It's an old brass miner's lamp. This round part was the reflector, see?"

"Julius Steincroft's lamp?"

"Could be."

So. Perhaps they were standing at the very spot where Lucy's father had met his death.

Mike scrambled up the face of the barrier.

Jodi heard her mother gasp. "Mike, come back here!"

"It's okay, Mom. Just want to test something . . ."

Mike wet his finger and held it up. "There's a current of air coming through at the top of these rocks!"

"You mean the tunnel goes on beyond here?" Billy questioned.

"I'm sure it does from the amount of tailings outside," answered his uncle. "Mines often branched several times to follow the veins of ore. I suspect Steincroft was starting a branch tunnel. There's too much rock here to have all fallen from the ceiling. Looks like part of it was blown into the main tunnel from the side."

Uncle Will posed the question that was on Jodi's mind. "How long do you think it would take to clear a passageway through to the other side of this rock pile?"

"That's hard to say. Didn't Miss Steincroft tell you the partners got discouraged and quit digging?" Mr. Marsh asked.

"She did, Dad," Mike called from his perch near

the ceiling. "She also said they didn't have money to carry on with the mining."

Despite her uneasiness, Jodi felt a great curiosity. "Can we try to make a hole through?"

"Well, I guess it won't hurt to try to see what's on the other side of these rocks. You kids will never let the matter die now."

Jodi almost forgot her claustrophobia. "Thanks, Dad! I'll dig first."

"No you won't," said Mike. "I'm already up here. But you can hold the light if you want."

So Jodi picked her way over broken rocks with the light while the others moved back, out of reach of the chunks that Mike tossed behind him.

When Mike got tired, Jodi took his place. The passage grew wider as the rocks rolled onto the tunnel floor.

"My turn now," called Billy.

Jodi slid down the loose rocks and groped her way back to the adults. Now that her mind wasn't occupied with work, the blackness of the mine pressed around her like a suffocating blanket.

They stood a while longer as the rocks come clattering down. Then Dad called a halt.

"Those batteries won't last much longer, kids. And it's getting late. Maybe tomorrow we can dig some more."

By the time they'd reached the creek at the foot of Morning Gulch, the sun had slid below the rim of the mountain, throwing a shadow across the valley.

Jodi stared into the leaping flames of the campfire that evening. What a day it had been! She gave a contented sigh. "We're missing the Fourth of July fireworks display on the waterfront tonight," she said. "But we have our own display . . . our fire, and look at all the sparklers in the sky!"

Above the trees a million stars traced a path of brilliant stepping stones across a black sky-river.

"It's beautiful, all right," agreed her father. "Jodi, where's our camp Bible? This is a good time for our family devotions."

Jodi ran inside the cabin and brought it to him. If Dad noticed that Uncle Will seemed uncomfortable, he didn't show it. Using a flashlight, he leafed through the pages. "Listen to this," he said. "Did you know that thousands of years ago, Job knew a lot about mining?" He began to read, skipping down through a long passage in the twenty-eighth chapter of Job:

> There is a mine for silver
> and a place where gold is refined. . . .
> Man puts an end to the darkness;
> he searches the farthest recesses
> for ore in the blackest darkness.
> Far from where people dwell he cuts a shaft,
> in places forgotten by the foot of man. . . .
> He tunnels through the rock;
> his eyes see all its treasures. . . .
> But where can wisdom be found? . . .
> It cannot be bought with the finest gold, . . .
> "The fear of the Lord—that is wisdom,
> and to shun evil is understanding."

Dad switched the flashlight off, but not before Jodi caught a puzzled expression on Billy's face.

"Anybody want to tell us what they think Job is saying here? Billy?"

"He's saying that men knew how to dig for gold way back then."

"True."

"He's talking about wisdom too, Dad," said Jodi. "He says it cannot be bought with finest gold."

"Also true. And what is wisdom?"

Mike spoke up. "He said the fear of the Lord is wisdom."

"That's right. I hope you kids will never forget that. No matter how much 'gold' you find in your lifetimes, you'll never be rich if God is not first in your lives."

Jodi thought about that. Uncle Will had scooted back into the shadows so she couldn't see his face, but Billy looked very thoughtful.

They began to discuss plans for the next day. Mike, Billy, and Jodi wanted to continue the excavation. Mrs. Marsh, of course, had to get back to Bayside for her afternoon's work at the bakery.

"I'll go with her back to the cabin so I can work on that car of yours," said Uncle Will. "I think it will be simple enough to fix, but if I'm wrong, Adele may have to come back after us."

"What do you think is wrong, Dad?" asked Billy.

"When you boys installed the distributor, remember, you seemed to be having some trouble with that timing light. If you weren't using it right you could have made a mistake in adjusting the setting. That would cause the engine to miss."

Jodi could tell that Billy felt embarrassed.

"Don't feel badly, Bill," his dad told him. "We brought the timing light along. If that's all it is, there's no problem. But I need someone to run the engine while I make adjustments and Adele will need to get to work."

"Then all three adults will have to go back to the valley," said Mr. Marsh. "You kids will have to wait until Will and I return to go back in the mine."

"But Dad!" protested Jodi. "That might not be 'til Saturday. We don't want to waste a whole day!"

Three pleading faces turned to him.

"Well, all right, if you'll promise to be extra careful. Stop if there's any sign of loose rock in the ceiling. And if you break through to the other side, will you promise to go no further until we get back?"

"Agreed!" they chorused.

With that decided, they put out the campfire and went to bed.

When Jodi woke the next morning the window left unshuttered at one end of the room showed gray. The air had gone out of her air mattress during the night and every muscle protested as she rolled over. Her mother was still asleep on Lucy's bed.

"Must be awfully early," she thought sleepily. She squinted again at the window as she sat up. No, it wasn't *that* early. The grayness came from clouds. Behind the cabin, mist swirled down over the mountain. The evergreens loomed out of the fog like dark ghosts.

Her mother stirred. "Morning, Jodi." She peered at her wristwatch. "Seven o'clock already?"

From below came sounds of a scuffle as Mike and the two men discovered that Billy had tied their shoes together in mismatched pairs the previous night. They heard a mighty protest from Billy as his covers were snatched away. Then Mike tossed Billy's shoes out the door in opposite directions. Billy picked his barefoot way after them with exaggerated moans.

Jodi and her mom came down the stairs.

"Get the fire going, boys. I'll mix some breakfast hotcakes," Mrs. Marsh announced.

"I'll fix the juice. And didn't we bring a can of bacon?" Jodi rummaged through the groceries in the cupboard for the powdered orange drink and the bacon. Billy picked up a kettle and headed to the creek for water while Mike started a fire. Soon coffee for the grown-ups simmered at the side of the campfire.

"How can anything that tastes as bad as coffee smell so good?" Jodi commented. She unwound the greasy parchment paper from the half-cooked canned bacon slices and separated them into a pan. Her mother poured tin cups of juice to pass around while the bacon sizzled.

They dug into the hotcakes with enthusiasm, eating them faster than Mrs. Marsh could cook them. Jodi finished hers and set down her plate. "I'll cook some now, Mom, while you eat."

As she worked she noticed that the gray sky looked brighter.

A short while later the three cousins waved as their parents headed toward the trail. "If we don't get back tonight, Will and I shall see you tomorrow," called Alan Marsh.

"Remember your promise," added his wife. "I want all three of you safe and sound when they get back."

Jodi waved once more and turned to the cabin. "We'd better take some food along to the mine. Wish we had some work gloves."

"We could put our socks over our hands," suggested Mike. "Or how about some of our dads' socks? They'd fit looser."

The men had left their bedrolls and extra clothing in the cabin. Mike picked out three pairs of heavy socks. "We can wash them tonight so they can wear them tomorrow," he said.

"Let's take our jackets. Even if the sun comes out, it's still cold in the mine," said Jodi.

They hiked briskly toward the upper end of the gulch, stopping once to rest.

A slight breeze made the fog lift and dip as if it were a living thing. "We're nearly into the clouds, aren't we?" remarked Billy. The billowy, gray-white underside hung almost low enough to reach up and touch. Jodi lay flat on her back in the grass, imagining ghosts of the past in the fog swirling along the side of the gulch. She shivered a little with the mystery of it.

Suddenly she gasped. One of her imaginings had soundlessly appeared out of the mist and stood less than twenty feet away, fixing them with a baleful glare. Still without a sound, the figure whirled and vanished.

Trapped!

Thunder lay facing away from the vanished apparition. But the hair along his neck stood on end. He got to his feet with a growl, every muscle tensed.

"Stay, boy." Billy's freckles popped out as if on stems. "Did you two see what I saw?"

"Yes. And I'm going after him." Mike leaped to his feet and strode toward the spot where the figure had disappeared. The other two followed close behind. Thunder stalked beside Billy, still growling. The fog grew thicker the higher they went. "Be careful," gasped Jodi.

"We'll never find him in this fog," said Mike.

Jodi pressed close to her brother, shivering at the memory of the stranger's angry glare. She tried to pull her startled impressions together. The stranger was wiry and short—not much taller than she or Billy. Fierce grizzled brows knit together in a face like old leather. A shapeless felt hat, a rusty gray beard, hair straggling to the collar of a ragged plaid jacket. High laced boots. One hand had clutched something at his shoulder; the strap of a backpack, maybe. She'd

111

glimpsed a heavy stick, like a cudgel, on which he leaned.

The two boys were talking in low voices. "Maybe Jodi was right about someone spying on us. I'll bet you anything it was that guy!" Billy whispered.

"But who is he?" asked Mike. "And why should he look so angry?"

"Remember what Miss Steincroft told us about old-timers still prospecting in these mountains?" asked Jodi. "Do you suppose that man is one of them?"

"He sure looked the part," Mike agreed.

Jodi stopped and faced her brother. "Oh, Mike, I'm scared. Maybe we should forget about working in the mine. At least 'til our dads get back."

Mike wavered. As the eldest, he was responsible for the others. But to let themselves be frightened away just because an old man frowned at them . . . His jaw set stubbornly.

"No. Let's go ahead with our plans. He's gone and probably won't be back. Remember, Miss Steincroft said that those old prospectors were harmless."

Jodi didn't remind him that she had said *most* of them were harmless. She just hoped that this one wasn't an exception. The cousins followed Thunder up the slope beside the tailing pile. At the mine's entrance they switched on their flashlights.

"Oh, nuts!" Billy shoved his light back into his pocket. "Should have put in fresh batteries. This one is almost dead."

"Batteries! I knew we were forgetting something! I meant to put some extras in with our lunch."

"We'll just have to make these last," said Mike.

"Put your flashlight away too, Jodi, 'til we really need it."

Oh no! Entering that tunnel *with* a light was bad enough. How could she go in there without one? Jodi swallowed hard and maneuvered herself between the two boys as they made their way along the tunnel.

Once they reached the rockfall, though, she almost forgot her fear.

The work was hard and dusty. Even with heavy wool socks over her hands, Jodi knew she had broken most of her fingernails. With her thumbs bound by the socks, she often lost her grip on a rock and dropped more than one on her toes. But their narrow passageway grew longer and deeper.

"Some of the rocks we're throwing back are landing inside the area we've already cleared. Let's try an assembly line," suggested Mike. They passed the rocks back from one to the other. The last person in line tossed the rocks out into the tunnel as far as he could.

"We might dig for a week and still get nowhere," complained Billy. "I'm hungry, and it's getting dark in here."

Jodi looked around apprehensively, but managed a giggle. "Dark in here! What do you expect inside a mine?"

Mike looked up from his crouching position at the head of the passageway. "It is darker. *My* batteries are going dead now. Why don't we stop for lunch? Then one of us could hike back for new ones."

They scrambled down the rock fall and made their way out of the tunnel. Thunder greeted them joyfully. Jodi felt just as joyful to be in the open again.

The midday sun blinded them at first. Jodi squinted up toward the pass. "I'm glad the fog lifted. And not a sign of that awful man, either."

Mike opened the packet of sandwiches. "This all we brought, Jodi? I could eat all these myself!"

"There's some dried fruit too. But I'll go after the extra batteries if you like, and bring back more food for this afternoon."

She finished her sandwich and swallowed the last of the fruit drink in her canteen. "I'll get more to drink too. Thunder can come with me, since he doesn't like the tunnel anyway. Anything else we need?"

"Just something to snack on, and the batteries, I guess," Mike decided. "And don't waste time, Jodi. We have only your light now."

As the boys returned to the tunnel, Jodi and the dog started down the gulch. The shade of the forest felt deliciously cool. Jodi stopped at the creek to scrub away the rock dust from her face and arms. She rinsed the canteen and filled it with fresh water.

Unlacing her boots, she stepped barefoot into the stream. "Ah, that feels good," she told Thunder, who was wading belly-deep beside the foot log.

Thunder climbed out onto the bank and galloped to where Jodi stood. He shook himself, splattering Jodi.

"You mutt!" she squealed. "You did that on purpose!"

Reluctantly she put her socks and boots on. At the cabin she dropped some purification tablets into the canteen. She rummaged among the groceries. "Rats! No more juice mix. We'll have to drink it like this." She shook the container to dissolve the tablets, then fastened it to her belt.

She pulled a plastic bag from the cupboard and put into it the flashlight batteries, some cheese, and some pilot bread. "I know we had some candy bars," she mumbled. "Oh, here they are." She stepped outside and whistled for Thunder.

"C'mon, boy. Mike and Billy will wonder what's keeping us." Jodi and Thunder crossed the creek and began the climb into Morning Gulch.

Suddenly, a muffled boom whooshed down the mountain. Jodi felt rather than heard it at first. Startled, she looked up. Echoes of the explosion came rolling after the shock wave. A cloud of dust hung in the air over the tailings.

Fear stabbed her heart. "Oh, dear Lord, what happened?" She began to run toward the mine, stumbling over hummocks of grass and around boulders, falling and running, until her breath tore her lungs and burned her throat. Thunder ran beside her, puzzled at her strange behavior.

Reaching the bottom of the tailings pile, Jodi tripped and fell once more. She lay gasping for air. As she lifted her head she saw a flash of red and black plaid on the wall above. The old man who'd glared at them this morning! The dog saw him too and growled.

"Sic him, boy," she hissed fiercely.

Thunder needed no urging. He'd smelled this scent before, and each time he'd sensed the concern of his young friends. Although he didn't know what fear caused Jodi to send him after the man, instinct prompted him to obey.

The prospector, unaware of Jodi and the dog, was crossing the hollow where Thunder had chased the pikas the day Jodi found the mine.

Suddenly he staggered back, for a snarling brown fury had launched itself over the edge of the tailings pile. The man threw his arms in front of his face just as sixty-five pounds of dog hit his chest and bore him to the ground. He cowered under the angry animal, feeling frantically for his walking stick.

At that moment Jodi appeared. She ran to Thunder and placed a restraining hand on his collar.

"All right, old man. Tell me right now, or I'll let Thunder at you again. What did you do to Mike and Billy?"

The prospector raised himself on one elbow. His greasy felt hat lay on the ground, his bald dome shining white above the fringe of long gray hair. His weather-browned face went pale.

"Mike? Billy? You—you—mean—the other two youngsters?" he croaked weakly. "You don't mean they were in the mine . . ." The old man struggled to a sitting position. "What have I done?"

Dark
Journey

Jodi followed the old miner to the tunnel entrance. She gasped. His blast had gouged a new cave above the old opening, which was now filled with shattered rock.

The man standing beside her frightened Jodi no longer. He seemed to shrivel before her very eyes. His face pinched and remorseful, he stammered out his story.

"Name's Jack McCracken, young lady. Been prospecting all my life. Heard stories about this fellow Steincroft long ago. Finally got a lead on the whereabouts of his diggings, but when I got here, I found you kids poking around. Didn't figure to hurt you none—just wanted to scare you away."

He lowered himself stiffly to a seat on a boulder. "When I came back after you saw me this morning, I found your packsack and those dirty old socks." He pointed to where they lay, just where Jodi had left them when she said good-bye to the boys. "I knew you'd been inside. I searched the gulch with my binoculars and saw you run into the woods down there. The brush was moving ahead of you and I heard you yell something. I figured the other kids were ahead of you."

"It was only Thunder." She choked back a sob.

His shoulders sagged even lower. "It's turned into a nightmare. The worst of it is, I didn't calculate right. Used way too much dynamite."

Jodi felt like wailing her despair. Were her brother and cousin hurt? Or dead under those tons of rock?

She dropped to her knees beside the old man and shook his arm. "Please, Mr. McCracken. Isn't there some way we can get to them?"

He raised his head slowly. "Y-e-s-s. There might be a way, if you're willing to help. A mine like this had to have air. Somewhere back of this cliff there should be an air shaft."

"How would that help?"

"We might be able to get into the tunnel through it."

Jodi felt the crushing weight of fear lift just a little. "There's no time to waste. Let's start looking."

With Thunder and the old man close behind her, she scrambled up the rib of rock beside the mine to the top of the wall. Stunted trees and bushes spread over the rocky plateau in front of them.

"The mine angles west and south." Jack Mc-Cracken pointed his walking stick. "The hole may be overgrown with brush, so watch your step."

Jodi broke a dead branch from a tree. She imitated her companion, swishing the stick ahead of her as she worked back and forth through the brush.

She pushed through the bushes and over rocks.

118

Soon she was panting. She began to shake violently in reaction to her fear. Dropping to the ground, crunchy with dry lichens, she put her head on her knees until the trembling lessened.

"God, please take care of the boys, whatever has happened to them," she whispered. "And, please Lord, if there's an air shaft, will You help us find it?"

Thunder whined and pushed his nose into her face. Some distance away, she could hear the old man's stick thrashing the brush. Jodi leaned her head against the dog's neck. "Oh, Thunder," she moaned. "How did all this happen? Why did I have to be so anxious to find this mine anyway?"

Then she sat up straight as something caught her eye. The ground before her dipped in a shallow bowl. And right in the center of the bowl, pushing up above the brush, were some square timbers, like those at the mine entrance.

"Mr. McCracken!" Her shout echoed.

Grabbing her stick, she flew across the uneven ground. Jack McCracken appeared at the rim of the depression.

"Stop, girl! You'll fall in if you don't watch what you're doing!"

The old man hastened to her. Cautiously they pushed ahead to where several timbers lay stacked helter-skelter atop each other. Jodi stepped up on the pile and caught her breath. Before her yawned a hole like the shaft of an elevator, straight down into the mountain.

The timbers had once formed some kind of shelter over the opening. The two picked their way around them to the bare rock on the opposite side of the hole. Jodi crept to the edge and looked down into blackness. She had batteries, but no flashlight. How could they ever look for the boys without a light? And how could they get down that hole anyway?

The prospector knelt beside her. He dropped a stone into the shaft. A moment later they heard a "thunk" as it hit bottom.

"Shaft seems to be clear, young lady. It's deep, but I think this will reach." He unfastened a coil of dirty rope from the side of his pack. He swiftly knotted a loop into one end of the rope. The other end he secured around a protruding chunk of bedrock.

"By rights it ought to be me going down there," he muttered. "But you're just a slip of a girl. You wouldn't be strong enough to pull me back up."

Jodi gulped. Since the time when, as a very small child she'd accidentally locked herself into a closet, she'd feared dark, enclosed places. Did this strange old man expect her to descend alone, without a light, into that hole? She couldn't!

Speechless, she watched the old man open his pack and take out a small brass object. It had two chambers, one on top of the other. She saw a hook on one side and a round reflector, something like the one on her dad's flash camera, on the other. Mr. McCracken poured some pungent-smelling chunks of a dusty white substance into one chamber.

"Hand me your canteen, young lady."

Jodi watched him carefully pour a little water into the other compartment. The water dripped slowly onto the white chunks. They began to bubble and fizz and he quickly screwed the top on. Next he turned a knob near the center of the reflector. This struck a spark, which ignited gas escaping from the hole in the reflector.

A flame leaped out. At the same time Jodi nearly choked with the sharp smell of the gas generated as water and chemical mixed. A carbide lamp! Like the smashed one they had found in the tunnel.

Jack McCracken looked critically at Jodi's sailor's cap. "That hat's no good to support this lamp. You'll have to carry it, but be careful not to drop it."

Jodi shuddered. Unable to protest, she watched as the old miner showed her how to step through the loop in the rope and use it as a kind of seat. She would have to hold the rope and the lamp with one hand, leaving the other free to keep herself from banging into the side of the shaft.

Her heart pounded as she sat down with the rope in place and dangled her legs over the edge of the shaft. "What am I doing?" she cried out to herself. "How do I

know he won't go away and leave me in the tunnel too? Oh, Lord . . . help me!"

The prospector wound the excess rope around the rock which anchored it. He stood beside the rock, holding the rope tight with both hands.

"All right, young lady. We'll take it very slowly. I'll let you down as easy as I can. When you're ready to come up, let me know by yanking on the rope."

Jodi turned on her side, pushing off with both hands, then reached up for the carbide lamp. She heard Thunder growl, then whine, as she disappeared into the hole. Good! He'd not let Mr. McCracken go off and leave her.

The rope cut into her thighs at the first sharp drop. She tried to kick away from the rock wall as she began to descend in slow jerks. The rope looked so old! What if it were to wear through on these rough rocks?

The lamp sputtered and stank. She leaned away from it as far as she could. The opening at the top of the shaft grew smaller and smaller. Where was the bottom? Chunks of dirt and rock loosened by the rope rattled over the side.

Just when she thought she would scream from terror, her toes touched the floor. She clung to the rope, shaking.

"I'm down!" Jodi called up toward the square of light. The prospector leaned over the edge of the hole. Toward the end of her descent, she had spun around several times. Now she had no idea in which direction the tunnel's mouth lay. But the man could see her in the glow of the carbide lamp.

"Turn around, young lady. Now, straight ahead. I'll wait right here—and good luck."

With a last despairing look toward the square of blue sky above her, Jodi stepped out into the blackness. The flickering flame of the lantern made shadows run over the rocky walls and ceiling. She followed the rusty rails on the floor, occasionally stepping over rocks. She dared not shout for fear of causing more rock to fall.

Once she had to step around an ore car, like the one they'd seen near the entrance. Then the rails divided, one set running back into a second tunnel on her right. She hesitated. Then, deciding that the mine entrance would be straight ahead, she went on.

Now and then she called the boys' names, softly. Only the echo of her own voice answered. She forced herself to move ahead. The walls and ceiling seemed to press closer.

"When I am afraid, I will trust in You." The words came quietly, like a comforting light.

"Yes, I do trust in You," Jodi whispered. "Help me, please Lord."

A rock rolled under her foot. Then her way was blocked by a heap of shattered rock. The other side of the rock fall! She held the carbide lamp high. There seemed to be a gap between the ceiling and the rocks. Had the boys broken through?

Jodi scrambled up to the passageway. Holding the carbide, she wiggled through and slid down the slope on the other side. Following the tunnel she came to the rocks shaken down by Mr. McCracken's dynamite. Not a sign of the boys. Were they under that rock?

Her courage fled. Jodi felt her face crumple and she wept aloud, shaking so that she had to sit down on the cold rock and set the lamp on the floor beside her. The flame sputtered, reminding her that her time to search was limited by the fuel in the lamp. She swallowed a sob.

She started back the way she'd come. Beyond the rock fall, she spied a discarded flashlight battery, then another. So their light was dead. Had they thrown the batteries away before or after the explosion?

At the fork of the tunnel she stopped. If the boys were alive, which way would they have gone? If they had seen the air shaft, they would have remained near it, she reasoned, so they probably had taken the other fork.

Jodi wanted with all of her heart to get out of the smothering darkness, back to that little square of blue light. But she made herself start down the unexplored passageway. Rivulets of water trickled down the walls, forming puddles along the sides. She tried to stay on the rails to keep her feet dry.

The floor sloped downward as she groped along. The air grew mustier. In one place a pocket of soft rock had crumbled and slid out into the tunnel, half-filling it. Jodi climbed over the barrier, expecting to see the end of the passageway.

"Michael! Billy! Are you here?" Her voice cracked as she called, loudly as she dared. How much farther? Her heart pounded. It took all the resolution she could muster to keep one foot moving ahead of the other.

Then the light sputtered and grew dimmer. "Oh no!" Jodi gasped. "Please, lamp, don't go out!"

Rescue

She would have to go back. She'd be very lucky if the lamp kept burning until she reached the air shaft. Once more she called, and this time used all the volume she possessed. She listened a moment, then turned to go.

What was that? Echoes? No! It was her own name being called, from far down the tunnel. With a sob of relief, Jodi rushed toward the calls.

"Jodi! Here! We're here!"

There, stumbling toward her, were two dirty, tired, but grinning boys. Jodi launched herself at her brother's neck and at that moment, the flame of her light shrank to pinpoint size and went out.

No one mentioned the darkness at first, in the babble of questions and explanations. Then Billy broke in. "How will we find our way to your air shaft without a light?"

"I think we could if we had to," replied Jodi. "But if you still have the flashlights, I have extra batteries."

"We have them," Mike answered. "We threw away two dead batteries just in case someone came looking for us—like Hansel and Gretel and the breadcrumbs, you know."

Jodi gave a shaky laugh. "I found two of them."

"We stopped when the other flashlight went dead," said Billy. "Jodi, if it hadn't been for you we could have starved to death in this tunnel."

"Do you suppose God planned for us to forget the extra batteries this morning?" Jodi asked. "If I'd been in the tunnel with you, and if our dads don't get back tonight, no one would have missed us until tomorrow. And even then they might not have thought about an air shaft."

While they talked, Jodi put two of the batteries from her sack into Mike's hand. By feel, he got them into the flashlight casing and put it back together. He switched on a flood of brightness which made all three of them blink.

Jodi dropped the carbide lantern into her sack, and brought out the candy bars. "Here you are, Billy. Now, tell me again—where were you boys when the dynamite went off?"

Mike put the batteries into the other flashlight and handed it to his cousin. "We'd just got through to the other side of the rockfall," he explained, "and we heard noises. We thought you were coming."

"We thought it would be fun to hide and make you think the old miner'd got us," said Billy.

"But we promised not to go past the rockfall," interrupted Jodi.

"Well, we didn't go far," he said. "But it's good we forgot our promise. We went down the tunnel 'til we came to a bulge in the wall. We scrunched up against the wall and turned the light out . . ."

"And all of a sudden there was this huge roar that knocked us down and nearly deafened us."

"I hit my head on a rock, or it hit me," said Billy.

"It was awful, thinking we might never get out of this mine!" exclaimed Mike. "Just wait until I get hold of that old man . . . what did you say his name is?"

"Jack McCracken," answered Jodi. "But Mike, remember, he didn't have to help me find you!"

They made their way along the tunnel. A thought began to nag at her. For all she knew, Mr. McCracken might never have intended to wait for her. He could be in a lot of trouble if people should learn what he had done.

Much sooner than she expected, they reached the fork in the tunnel. They passed the ore car, and a few minutes later they stood beneath the air shaft. A small white cloud floated across the opening. Jodi gave the dangling rope a tug. Nothing happened. She pulled harder.

Just as she feared. He was gone! Jodi threw back her head, cupped her hands to her mouth and yelled, "Mr. McCracken! Mr. McCracken!"

They heard a bark. Then Thunder poked his head over the edge of the shaft. Jodi could tell from the way his one drooping ear swung back and forth that his wagging tail was about to propel him over the edge.

"Fool dog! Get back!" Jack McCracken's black felt hat and leathery face appeared in the opening. The old prospector's expression of relief was comical to see.

127

"Glory be, youngster! You're back. I was afeard you'd gone and lost yourself too. I see you found them."

"Can you get us out, Mr. McCracken?" Jodi shouted up.

"Don't you fret. I've put together a contraption that'll have you out in no time. I'll need the lightest one of you up here first. Who'll it be?"

"Me, I guess." Jodi glanced at the boys. She stepped into the rope sling.

"Ready?" The miner's face disappeared. A moment later Jodi felt the rope tighten and lift. Clinging to it, she walked her feet up the wall as the rope jerked her higher. A few minutes later she rolled over the edge, into the sunshine.

Thunder leaped at her with slurps and wiggles. Crawling away from the hole, she sat up and caught him in her arms. Good old Thunder! She thought she would cry with the joy of just being alive and free of the terror that had gripped her down in the mine. Then she noticed Mr. McCracken working with the rope a few paces away.

"Mr. McCracken! What an *ingenious* invention!" Ingenious was a word Jodi had never tried aloud before, but it did fit the prospector's "contraption" perfectly. He had taken a smooth, barkless section of dead tree, about eight inches thick, and wedged one end between some outcrops of rock. The other end he had braced behind the small tree he had used when he let Jodi down into the mine.

The rope wound once around the log before passing over the edge of the air shaft. Then as he pulled on his end of the rope, the log turned, like a pulley, helping to lessen the force needed to bring up the load on the other end.

The prospector tossed the rope into the shaft again. Jodi sprang to help him, both of them hauling hand over hand on the upper end. In a few moments, Billy tumbled over the edge. Mr. McCracken paused to cut out and reknot a badly frayed section of rope, and then it was Mike's turn to scramble out. Thunder gave each boy the same welcome he'd given Jodi.

Jodi's legs suddenly felt weak. She plopped on the ground beside the boys. The three were a dirty, bedraggled lot, with muddy clothes and shoes. A trickle of dried blood ran down the side of Billy's face where the rock had struck him during the explosion.

An awkward silence stretched between the young people and the prospector, now coiling his rope. Jodi decided to make introductions.

"Mr. McCracken, this is my brother Mike and our cousin Billy."

The man grunted. Now that they were safe, he looked as if he couldn't decide whether to remain angry at the intruders or to fear the consequences of his action. His relief at their rescue won out.

"You three look as tuckered as I feel. I'm going to put my coffee pot on. Maybe a good cup of brew will perk us all up."

None of the cousins drank coffee, but they did not say so. They watched as the prospector brushed debris off a slab of rock and expertly kindled a tiny fire, feeding it bits of dry wood until a nice little blaze crackled. He took a blackened coffee pot from his pack, shook some

129

coffee grounds into it, and poured in water from his canteen.

"Shucks!" he muttered. "That wasn't enough."

"Here, Mr. McCracken. Use the water in my canteen." Jodi handed it to him.

He set the pot on three stones, just over the flame. A thin line of smoke rose into the air as he continued to add one small piece of wood at a time. Soon the water boiled. The aroma of coffee swirled around them. And when Mr. McCracken brought out an assortment of battered metal cups and bowls and offered some to each, they accepted it gratefully.

Jodi sipped hers slowly. The bitter hot liquid warmed her clear to her toes, and her energy began to return. "Mr. McCracken," she said. "I told the boys that you didn't know they were in the mine and that you only wanted to scare us away. But how did you know about the lost mine in the first place?"

The old man wiped his sleeve across his moustache.

"Well, you know how us old-timers are, young lady. We swap stories every time two of us get together. Years ago many people knew of Steincroft's mine, but lots of holes were dug in this country, and gradually people forgot where his was. I worked up north for years and years—came back to this country to retire. But after spending my whole life searching and never finding much, I still had the gold fever."

The black eyes under the grizzled brows were far away with remembering. "Why," thought Jodi, "Mom was right when she said that inside everybody, no matter how different he may seem, is a real human being.

Mr. McCracken might have killed us, but I can't help liking him."

He went on. "That was a couple of years ago. One day I was out roaming the hills when I remembered hearing the old story about Steincroft. He lived before my time, but rumors like that don't die out easily. And rumor was that he thought he had struck it rich.

"I decided to look for his diggings, though I wasn't sure where to look. I happened into this gulch one day a month or so ago. Found a couple of prospect holes; had taken shelter in the one behind the cabin the day of the big storm, matter of fact, when I saw you three come out of the woods like drowned rats.

"I finally found the mine. When you came back again and started fooling around in the gulch, I knew you had found it, too, and would bring in a swarm of curious flatlanders before I could stake my claim. I didn't know you knew about Steincroft. I just wanted to scare you away!"

"Then it was *your* footprint we found in the tunnel near the cabin!" Jodi exclaimed.

"And the light flashing in Billy's eyes, that almost made him fall down the cliff—did you have anything to do with that?" Mike demanded.

The old man looked startled. "Not on purpose. I saw him slip, but I didn't know why. If something flashed in his eyes, maybe it was the sun reflecting from my pick." He motioned to his pack, with the shiny tool tied on the outside. "Durn careless of me," he muttered to himself.

"Why were you spying on us anyway? Why didn't

131

you come talk to us, find out what we wanted?" Mike asked.

The old man sighed. "I should have. I should have. I came mighty close to killing you boys, and I've lost my chance at the mine anyway!"

"Maybe not, Mr. McCracken," Jodi countered. "We couldn't work the mine ourselves. Maybe somehow *you* could open it up. Especially when we tell you what we know about the mine. Okay if we tell him, boys?"

"Guess so." Mike and Billy nodded. So the three of them told the whole story, beginning with Jodi's discovery of the treasure bag. A sparkle came to the old man's eyes as they told him of the nuggets, and the ore in the stable.

"Would take a lot of work, a lot of time," he began.

Just then Thunder, who had been lying quietly beside Billy, leaped up with a happy "whoof" and trotted off toward the rim of the depression.

And there, against the sky, looking scared, angry, and relieved all at the same time, stood Alan Marsh and Will Skarson.

Birth
of an Idea

Jodi scrambled to her feet. "Dad! Uncle Will! What are you doing *here*?"

"What are *you* doing here?" Mr. Marsh demanded. "You kids scared the socks off of us. Somebody's got some explaining to do, and quick!"

Jodi gulped. She had never seen her tall, easygoing father so upset. He strode toward them, his flashing eyes on the weatherbeaten stranger kneeling speechless beside the fire. Right behind came stocky, sandy-haired Uncle Will, grim-faced as her father.

Mr. Marsh had asked for a quick explanation, and the three took him at his word. They all began to talk at once.

"We tunneled through the barrier . . ." began Mike.

"Dad, you'll never believe the way we got out . . ." Billy interrupted.

"It was all a mistake," babbled Jodi. "Mr. Mc-Cracken wasn't trying to hurt anyone . . ."

133

"Wait a minute. One at a time. Mike, you tell us what happened."

So Mike began with Jodi's departure to fetch more food and batteries, their clearing a way over the rockfall, and the explosion which trapped them in the tunnel. Jodi broke in to tell how she and Thunder had caught the prospector, and how he had helped her rescue the boys.

The old man hunched over the embers of the fire. Will Skarson growled, "Setting off that dynamite was crazy! We ought to have you arrested, mister."

"Oh no, Uncle Will!" Jodi exclaimed. "He only meant to frighten us away. If it hadn't been for him, I'd never have found the boys! It was his idea to look for the airshaft. And he thought of the way to get us out."

Mr. Marsh still looked pale, but he had regained his self-control. He squatted between Mike and Jodi, and the rest sat down too. "Well, I won't scold you boys for going beyond the rockfall. From what you say, you hadn't intended to do any exploring, and being beyond it probably saved your lives, thank God!" He changed the subject. "Tell us, Mr. McCracken, what is *your* interest in the mine?"

The old man repeated the story he had told the young people. "I guess I just got carried away, hoping for one last big strike." His shoulders slumped dejectedly as he mumbled into his grizzled beard, "Guess this is the end of my prospecting days. When I get so greedy I hurt innocent people, it's time to quit."

No one answered. Jodi felt sorry for old prospector,

134

but she knew that the two fathers still had mixed feelings toward him.

Mike thought of something else. "How did you know where we were, Dad?" he asked. "Didn't you say you wouldn't be back until tomorrow? It *is* still Friday, isn't it?"

Jodi, too, felt time had telescoped. Had it really been only that morning that their parents hiked away from the Steincroft cabin?

"Didn't take long to fix Eliza," answered Alan Marsh. "Will can tell you about that later. We thought we'd come back and help you dig. But when we got to the mine and found it caved in . . . well, you'll never know how we felt until you have kids of your own." He put an arm around each of his youngsters. "Anyway, we saw scrapes and dislodged pebbles where someone had climbed over the rocks next to the mine. We climbed up the same way, saw the smoke, and came right to you."

Uncle Will stood up. "Alan, these kids look bushed. I think we'd better get them to the cabin for some supper and a good night's sleep."

"I agree," answered Jodi's father. "Mr. McCracken, I'm sorry we didn't meet under happier circumstances. I want you to know that we're grateful for your help in rescuing the kids. Will you join us at the cabin for breakfast tomorrow?"

"Thanks," the prospector answered gruffly. "Maybe I will. And if we're going to get better acquainted, I answer best to 'Jack.' Don't cotton much to that 'Mr. McCracken' stuff."

Everyone stood up.

Jodi took a few steps, then turned back. "Mr. McCrack—I mean, Jack, where will you sleep tonight?"

"Don't worry about me, young lady. Got me a little pup tent in my pack. Right here's as good a place as any to spend the night."

Jodi looked back as they reached the rim of the depression. The miner once more stooped over his fire, fanning the embers back to life. She turned and trudged after the others.

Back at the cabin, Jodi collapsed against the wall. Her head whirled, and every muscle ached. The boys flopped to the ground too. They looked as weary as she felt.

"What have we got to fix for supper, Jodi?" Mr. Marsh asked. "No, you stay there. Just tell me what to look for."

"There's some dehydrated soup in the cupboard inside. And cheese and bread. How about toasted cheese sandwiches?"

While Uncle Will kindled a fire, her father found the food. Soon a pot of soup bubbled over the flames, and cheese sandwiches broiled in a fry pan.

"It's delicious, Dad," Jodi mumbled after a few bites, "but I'm just too tired to eat. Do you mind if I turn in now?"

"Go ahead, Jodi. But your mom would never let you go to bed with such a dirty face."

"Oh, I forgot! If I look as bad as Billy and Mike, I guess I do need a wash."

Thunder escorted her to the creek, where a good splashing with the cold water didn't wake her up much. Back in Lucy's room she unrolled her sleeping bag on the little bedframe, too tired to inflate her air mattress. As her thoughts swirled toward sleep, she managed to whisper, "Thank You, Father. I trusted You . . . You helped me."

The next morning the sun, rising over the ridge east of the cabin, sent a shaft of brightness through the window. It struck full in Jodi's face. She clenched her eyelids tightly against the light and lay enjoying the warmth of the sun on her cheek. But she sat up when Thunder growled and picked his way down the stairs. He stood by the closed door and continued to growl.

Jodi squirmed from her sleeping bag and tiptoed to the stairs. "Quiet, Thunder," she hissed. "You'll wake everybody!"

Glancing out the window she saw what had upset the dog. Jack McCracken sat waiting on the roots of a clump of trees across the clearing.

"Good morning! Have you been here long?" she called.

"Just got here. Should have known you folks might feel like sleeping in this morning."

Jodi heard stirrings from below.

"We'll be right out."

As she pulled on a sweatshirt and ran a comb through her tangled hair, she thought, "Sleeping in! My goodness! The sun just came up. I wouldn't call that sleeping in."

The boys went outside. Hearing exclamations of admiration, she looked out the window to see the prospector holding up a string of fat rainbow trout. They were so fresh, water still glistened on their sides.

Jodi mixed pancake batter while her father fixed

a pot of cocoa and another of coffee. The boys helped Jack McCracken clean the trout. Soon they were all satisfying appetites that had revived amazingly. Billy polished off his last flapjack and set his empty plate atop the stack of dirty dishes. "Best breakfast I ever ate!"

"Thanks to the fish," said Jodi. "Flapjacks by themselves get pretty tiresome."

"In my kind of business one sometimes eats flapjacks three times a day. Can't afford to get tired of them," answered the old miner. "But I agree with young Red. Mighty fine breakfast!"

"Well, we're glad you came, Jack, and we thank you for the trout." Alan Marsh poured himself another cup of coffee.

The old miner stood up and pushed back his hat, exposing the pale scalp above his brown face. He fidgeted a little, then squatted on his heels again.

"You know," he said, "I did a lot of thinking last night. These are fine kids here. And they did get into the mine first. Was thinking—if they wanted to go shares on what we might find, I'd be proud to have their help in opening up the mine."

No one said anything for a moment. Jodi glanced across the fire to the two boys. Their expressions mirrored her own. To spend the summer working a real mine! What if—what if—they found the vein from which the gold in the stable had come? And what if it contained a lot more of the same? She looked pleadingly at her father.

"That's very kind of you," he said slowly. "But I'm sure Will agrees with me. That's heavy, dangerous work. Besides, when my wife finds out what happened as soon as she turned her back on these three, she's apt to never let them out of her sight again."

Jodi saw the relief on the prospector's face.

"Thought I'd make the offer anyway. I can do it on my own. It'll take a little longer, but I've got plenty of time. You *will* let the youngsters visit sometimes?"

Both fathers nodded.

"I'd better be on my way then." They rose to their feet. "My base camp's thirty miles east of here. It's a long hike back. Got to pack up my things to move to the gulch. Then I'll have to take a trip to town for more provisions and to register my claim. By the way, I'd appreciate you keeping the story quiet for a few days. Not too many claim jumpers around these days but you can't be too careful!"

"We'll keep it quiet. Good luck!" they called after him.

"Suspicious old guy, isn't he?" Uncle Will chuckled when Jack McCracken was well out of hearing.

"Yes," answered Jodi's dad. "Just doesn't seem to realize the time is past for individuals on their own to make a living at mining. I don't think he'd have much competition for the claim even if the whole country knew about it."

"Oh, we know, Dad," Jodi nodded. "But how many kids our age ever have a chance to be partners in a working mine? And just helping would have been a real adventure."

"You've had a real adventure. And I hope you never have another one like it, Daughter. Now everybody fall to. Let's get packed up and on our way."

"All right. Who'll help me carry these dishes down to the stream?"

With the dishes clean, each person repacked his own load. The boys dug a hole and buried the non-burnable garbage, then sprinkled water over the ashes of the fire. Soon the work was done, and all the campers, with Thunder frisking ahead, started toward the trail.

Jodi came last. As she reached the edge of the clearing, she turned to look back at the little log house with its mountain backdrop and the trees towering beside it. Mike and Billy stopped too.

Jodi sighed as she turned to them. "This is such a special place. I wish it could always stay the same!"

"Me too," answered Mike. "But it won't, you know. Once people notice that the trail is being used, they'll follow it just to see what's there, and it won't be long before vandals will have the cabin torn to pieces."

"Oh, I couldn't stand that!" Jodi cried. "I'd like other people to be able to come here, and learn, and enjoy themselves, like we did. But there must be *some* way to keep it from being ruined."

The two fathers, finding themselves alone on the trail, had backtracked in time to overhear her words.

There was silence for a moment as they all stood looking at the cabin drowsing in the sun, a living part of the history of the great Pacific Northwest.

"You know," Alan Marsh said thoughtfully, "maybe there is a way, Jodi."

Home

"What do you mean?" Everyone turned to the tall, dark history teacher.

"Lucy's cabin—the mine too, perhaps—I'm pretty sure—they would qualify for protection as historical sites."

"Historical sites?" repeated Uncle Will. "Like some of those famous old buildings back east that have been fixed to look like they did in the early days?"

"Yes."

"That's a wonderful idea!" Jodi's mind leaped ahead to another possibility. "Dad, didn't you tell us that the county schools are planning to build an outdoor education camp near our summer cabin?"

"Yes. Just a few miles downriver. It'll be ready by next spring."

"Wouldn't Morning Gulch be a great place to bring the campers when they study about resources in this area?"

"That would be a perfect field trip!" exclaimed Mike. "And the cabin could show visitors how early settlers lived."

"Why don't you go to see Mrs. Neileson at the library when we get back to Bayside," suggested Mr. Marsh. "She'd know what steps to take. You're right, Jodi. Lucy's cabin and Morning Gulch should be kept for everyone to enjoy."

Jodi swung lightly along the trail, her mind abuzz with all that had happened since the weekend Billy and his father came to live with them.

"I'll visit Lucy first thing next week," she planned. "Won't she be happy to know that her old home might help people know what pioneer living was really like?"

Some time later the old green Ford rolled along toward Bayside. "What do you think of Eliza now, kids?" asked Alan Marsh.

"Runs as well as she ever did!" answered Mike. "By the way, Uncle Will. What caused the missing and the backfiring?"

Uncle Will twisted around to grin at the three sitting behind him. "Oh, nothing much," he said with a twinkle in his eyes. "The distributor was badly out of adjustment, but it didn't take long to reset it. Remember, I suspected that was what was wrong."

Billy looked embarrassed. "Then it *was* my fault, Dad. But I thought we did it just the way you've showed me."

"You did, Son. You just forgot to check the setting of the points before you started, that's all."

"Nobody's complaining, Billy," said his uncle. "You boys did a fine job, according to your dad. Thanks to

142

the Skarsons, Eliza's almost as good as new, and we won't have to buy another car this year."

Jodi remembered her fears of a dull summer vacation. "Just think of all the adventure we've already had this summer," she said. "And there's still half the vacation left!"

She settled back in her seat to watch the countryside moving past the window. Unbidden, a picture came to mind of the night they'd taken refuge from the storm in Lucy's cabin.

"Lord, You did it, didn't You?" Jodi thought."You brought Billy to live with us. You took care of the broken-down car, You took care of us in the storm and in the mine—You helped us find Lucy. Everything *is* working together for good. Thank You, God."

The car slowed to enter the city. Soon they pulled up in front of the big white house that was now home for both families. The cousins spilled out of the station wagon and into the house, Thunder at their heels. Mrs. Marsh, looking cool and neat in a blue-checked dress, met them in the hall .

"Hello, everybody! I've been expecting you." She took a closer look at the three dirty campers. "Jodi! Mike! Billy! To the showers, and don't forget to wash your hair. There's a big bowl of crab salad in the refrigerator as soon as you're clean. And Thunder, out! You don't belong in the house!"

Billy and Thunder scuttled out the back door and down to their apartment. Jodi hurried upstairs to shower while Mike helped the men unload the camping equipment. She towel-dried her hair, pulled on clean jeans and T-shirt, and padded barefoot down the stairs.

"It's all yours, Mike."

Her mother stirred the cocoa simmering on the stove. "Well, dear, did you have a good time?"

Jodi hesitated. How should she answer that question? "Just about the most exciting time ever, Mom." She put the toaster on the table and set plates around. Soon everyone dug in to heaps of chilled Crab Louis, buttery hot toast, and mugs of cocoa.

Before long Mrs. Marsh had pried out the details of their adventure at Morning Gulch, and Jodi waited nervously for her mother's reaction.

"Thank God you're all right!" she said at last. "That awful man! Alan, I think he ought to be locked up. Right away!"

"Now, Adele. I'm convinced he didn't intend to harm the kids. Don't forget, he helped Jodi get the boys out of the mine. And he did try to make amends. I'm sure he's learned his lesson."

"But didn't you children have any clue that he was watching you?"

The three cousins gulped. This was a part of the story they had left out before.

"Yes . . . Friday morning, before we went into the mine, we saw him . . ."

"Saw him!" Now it was Mr. Marsh's turn. "Did you talk to him?"

"No, he disappeared in the fog. We couldn't find him."

"We thought he'd gone away," added Jodi. "We had no idea he knew about the mine too."

"I guess it was really my fault that we got into trouble," admitted Mike. "After we saw Jack disappear in the fog, Jodi wanted to wait until the grown-ups got back to go into the mine. I was the one who said that we should go ahead."

"That's a switch," said his father. "Usually it's Jodi who leaps before she looks."

"Well, she sure kept her head yesterday," said Mike. "You should have seen her, Mom. Even though she's scared of closed-in places, she went down into that mine all alone to find us."

Jodi glowed at her brother's praise. "I didn't do it by myself. I prayed. I *really* prayed. And I felt like Jesus came and walked beside me while I was looking for the boys." She added, "I don't think feeling shut-in will bother me as much anymore."

"Oh, I hope so, Jodi," said her mother. "If we just remember that Jesus is a friend who never leaves us, we can face anything."

Billy listened intently. Then his face broke into a grin as his aunt continued. "I've changed my mind about something. After hearing how Thunder tackled that man, I'm never going to chase your dog out of the house again!"

Uncle Will had seemed uncomfortable at the talk of Jesus. He fastened upon the change of subject. "Going back to Jack McCracken and the mine," he said. "How did he find it? He must have been watching you before."

"Yes, he was," said Mike. "He'd already found the mine, and he was afraid we'd find it too. But we didn't know he was watching. Though the second time we came to the cabin, Jodi suspected someone had been there while we were gone."

"And we found a heelprint in the prospect hole behind the cabin," said Jodi.

"And Jodi saw something move in the woods that time I fell . . ." Billy stopped. This was something else they hadn't mentioned. Jodi quickly began to talk about their idea of getting the cabin and Gulch set aside as an historical site.

The two families sat around the table until long after dark, talking. Finally Jodi said good-night. Getting into her pajamas, she wriggled down into her soft blankets. Lucy's little wooden doll sat propped against the bedside lamp. Jodi picked her up and looked into the smiling painted face.

"Lottie, wait 'til your mistress hears what we have to tell her this time!"

A Beginning,
An Ending

Next morning, Sunday, Jodi woke to the sound of rain beating on the roof. Before breakfast she ran downstairs to ask hopefully, "Uncle Will, are you and Billy coming to church with us today?"

"Not today," her uncle replied. "I've got to clean our apartment. Billy can go if he wants to."

Alan Marsh brought Eliza to the front of the house. Everyone rushed through the downpour to scramble in.

"Your dad hasn't come to church with us since you came to Washington, Billy. Why won't he come?" asked Jodi.

"He used to go with Mom and me. When she didn't get well, I know I was mad at God. Maybe Dad still feels that way."

Mrs. Marsh smiled over her shoulder, a little sadly. "I think you're right, Billy. We'll just keep praying that someday your dad will know how much God really loves him." Jodi nodded.

On Monday, Jodi had planned to go see Lucy at

the nursing home. But the rain kept falling. It rained Tuesday too.

On Tuesday morning Mike cleaned the garage for his dad, while Jodi helped Billy review social studies and English lessons. But she could tell Billy wasn't concentrating.

"Let's stop for some milk and cookies," she suggested.

Billy's freckled face was serious as he took the glass she offered. "I've been thinking, Jodi. Your mom talks about Jesus in our lives. And you said when you were in the mine, it was like He was walking right beside you. How can somebody who is in heaven be in you, or beside you?"

"Oh, Billy—not everybody in heaven can be beside you!"

"I know that. My mother is in heaven. I wish she could be beside me, but I know she can't."

"You see, Billy," Jodi explained. "When Jesus went back to heaven, He sent His Spirit to live in everyone who believes in Him and loves Him."

"Does His Spirit live in you?"

"Yes, because I'm a Christian. And when I die, I'll go to heaven where Jesus is."

"I don't understand—how come you're so sure you'll go to heaven?"

"I know that Jesus died to take the punishment for the things I do wrong. And because God raised Him from the dead, I get to go to heaven when I die."

"That's all?"

"That's all. Billy, do you believe in Jesus?"

Jodi opened the big Bible on the coffee table. She

turned the pages until she found the spot she was looking for. "See this verse? John 3:16 . . . it says that God loved the world so much that He gave His Son, so that anyone who believes in Him will not die but have eternal life."

"I learned that verse when Mom and Dad used to take me to Sunday school."

"It's true, Billy. Jesus did die for you. Do you believe in Him?"

"Yes . . . I do," Billy said thoughtfully.

"Then tell Him so," said Jodi.

Billy closed his eyes and bowed his head like the others did when they prayed. "Jesus, I really do believe You died for me. I'm sorry for the things I've done wrong. I'm glad You're a part of my life, just like you are for Mike and Jodi. Amen."

"Amen," said Jodi.

That night at dinner, Jodi and Billy told everyone about their talk. Mrs. Marsh's face shone as she hugged her nephew. Billy's dad said nothing, but Jodi noticed a shadow of pain in his eyes. He disappeared to the basement apartment as soon as the meal ended.

Wednesday noon the sun finally came out.

"I think Lucy would like to hear what happened to us last weekend," Jodi said to the boys. "Want to go visit her this afternoon?"

"We're going fishing down at the waterfront, Jodi," Mike replied. "You go ahead. We'll come next time."

So Jodi caught the bus and skipped alone up the steps to the big coral-trimmed building. The lounge seemed cool and dim after the brightness outside. Jodi paused, blinking, as she looked for Mrs. Kratz. Then she saw her coming down the hall.

"Hello, Mrs. Kratz," Jodi said cheerfully. "I've come to visit Miss Steincroft."

"Fine, Jodi. I know she'll be happy to see you. You must stay only a few minutes, though."

"What's the matter? Is she sick?" Jodi interrupted anxiously.

"Yes, she's been quite ill, Jodi. She had a heart attack. She's in a private room now where she can have more rest."

An elevator took them to the second floor. Down a hall they turned into a room where the old lady lay propped on pillows. She looked even smaller than before.

She turned her head as Jodi tiptoed in. A smile lit her worn face. She held out a shaking hand. "You did come back," she whispered.

"Only a few minutes now," Mrs. Kratz reminded. She hurried off down the hall.

Jodi took the fragile hand. "How are you, Miss Steincroft?"

"Better, thank you. Tell me, did you find the mine?"

"Yes, we found it. But someone else did too." Jodi told the old lady about the prospector who wanted to reopen the mine. She left out the part about the boys being trapped by the dynamite explosion, not wanting to upset her. "Mr. McCracken asked us to help him, but our parents said we can't. You don't mind if he opens the mine, do you, Miss Steincroft?"

"Oh, indeed not. But he'll be fortunate if the mine pays for itself, don't you know?"

"We had a marvelous idea . . ." Jodi quickly told Lucy of their hopes that the cabin and surroundings could be preserved. "Someone would be there to take care of it. Visitors could hear the story of your family and learn about mining in the early days. What do you think, Miss Steincroft?"

The tired eyes brightened. "A wonderful idea. Perhaps I'm just a vain old lady, but who could ask for a better memorial? In a way I could go right on helping people learn, don't you know, even after I'm gone."

"Oh, Miss Steincroft. I want you to get well."

"There's nothing to be afraid of, Jodi. A wise person once said that death is a door, not a wall. I've enjoyed a good life, but when God calls me, I'll be ready to see what's on the other side of that door."

Mrs. Kratz stepped to the sick woman's side. "Time is up, Jodi."

Jodi bent to kiss her friend. "Good-bye, Miss Steincroft. Please, get better soon."

Lucy patted her cheek. "Thank you for coming, dear."

Jodi soberly followed Mrs. Kratz to the elevator. "When may I come back, Mrs. Kratz?"

"Why don't you leave your telephone number? When she's a little stronger, I'll give you a call."

Jodi left her number at the desk and went out to the stop to wait for the bus. She felt heavy-hearted. What if Lucy should die? Everyone died sometime, but Lucy was her *friend*.

That evening Jodi answered questions about her

visit to the nursing home with only a subdued yes or no. Mrs. Marsh looked at her sharply. Such lack of enthusiasm wasn't like Jodi.

That evening at bedtime, Jodi sat in her pajamas thinking, knees drawn up to her chin. Mrs. Marsh tapped on the door and entered at Jodi's "Come in." She sat down on the bed next to her daughter.

"Jodi, did something go wrong this afternoon?"

"Oh, Mom," Jodi burst out. "Miss Steincroft is awfully sick! She might die!"

"I'm sorry to hear that." Mrs. Marsh put her arm around Jodi's shoulders. "Does it frighten you to think of her dying?"

"I-I—guess so. She's my friend, Mom!"

"I understand how you feel. The hardest thing on earth is to lose someone you love. But aren't you glad you've had the chance to know her?"

"Yes-s-s, I am. Even if we'd never known about the cabin and the mine and all that, I'm still glad we got acquainted. I never had a really *old* friend before." Jodi smiled a little.

"People are people, no matter what their age."

"Yes, that's one of the things I learned from her. Do you think I'll be as brave and cheerful as she when I get to be old, Mom?"

"I'm sure you will. Do you know why? You and Miss Steincroft both know that for those who love God, dying is only the beginning of 'real' living."

"A door," murmured Jodi. "She said death is a door."

The girl lifted her head. "Anyway, she was pleased

about our ideas for the cabin. I'm going to pray for her. Maybe God *will* help her get better."

"Good-night, Sweetheart. I hope He does. I'm anxious to get to know her too."

"Mom, Mrs. Kratz said she'd call when I could come back again. Maybe we can both go!"

"I'd like that. Now, try to go to sleep."

Jodi scooted under the covers and switched off her light. That night she dreamed of a white-haired old lady hiking along a trail behind a pack mule. As they came to a tumbling mountain stream the old lady turned into a barefoot little girl with a long skirt and pigtails. The little girl ran laughing through the sparkling water. She vanished and so did the dream, and when Jodi woke it was morning.

Lucy's Bequest

The next few days passed quickly. Jodi and the boys went to see Mrs. Neileson, the librarian. The brisk little lady listened closely as they brought her up to date on their adventures at the gulch. Then they told her of their hopes for preserving the cabin and its surroundings.

"We know you are interested in local history, Mrs. Neileson," Jodi finished. "So we thought you might know what we should do."

"Perhaps I can help," smiled the librarian. "Did you know I am the president of the Bayside Historical Society? The society may be interested in taking your idea as a project. We might even be able to sponsor the restoration of the cabin."

The cousins grinned at each other. This *was* good news!

"I'll tell you what," she continued. "Our regular meeting is next week. I'll prepare a proposal for the society, and let you know what they decide."

A week later the phone rang for Jodi. Mrs. Neileson's energetic voice crackled in her ear.

"Well, Jodi—we're underway! The society likes the project you three suggested. Of course, there's much to be done before we can make a definite decision, but from what you told us, Morning Gulch holds a bit of history that really should be preserved. We've appointed a committee to visit the cabin to see what needs to be done. Someone will call you soon to invite you and the boys to guide them to the spot. Would you like to do that?"

Would they! Jodi's head whirled.

She danced back to the kitchen, where she and Billy had been loading the supper dishes into the dishwasher.

"Let's get this finished," she told him. "I've got news to tell everybody as soon as we're done." She pulled a couple of plates from the dishwasher and handed them back to her cousin. "You've got to rinse these cleaner."

"Slave driver," he grumbled.

"Just be glad we don't have to heat our water on a wood stove and wash dishes in a pan like Miss Steincroft did when she was a girl!"

The doorbell sounded. Jodi heard Mike open the door. "Hello, Mike." It was Mrs. Kratz.

When she saw the distress on the face of the usually cheerful nurse, Jodi knew why she had come.

"It's Miss Steincroft, isn't it?"

"I'm sorry, Jodi. Yes, she died this afternoon. I wanted to tell you myself." Mrs. Kratz held out an envelope and a package. "She wanted you to have these."

To Jodi it seemed as if those in the room stood frozen in place. She found her voice. "No!" she cried. "I don't believe it." She pounded up the stairs and slammed the door of her room.

The tears came. "Why, God?" she sobbed. "Miss Steincroft—Lucy—was my friend!"

She reached for the box of tissues next to the bed. Lottie sat there smiling. Jodi clasped the little doll close. Through her weeping she seemed to hear someone say softly, "I am Lucy's friend too. She is with Me now."

Jodi remembered the envelope and package. She blew her nose and went back downstairs. Mrs. Kratz had gone. The tears started again when she saw her name written in Lucy's old-fashioned handwriting.

"Don't cry, Jodi." Billy handed her a rumpled tissue from his back pocket. "Miss Steincroft isn't sick or hurting anymore. She loved Jesus. So she's safe in heaven." He paused. "Do you suppose she's met my mother yet?"

Mrs. Marsh answered softly, "I wouldn't be a bit surprised if they're sitting together under a shady tree somewhere in heaven, and your Mom is asking all kinds of questions about her little boy."

Jodi brightened. "I can just hear Miss Steincroft saying, 'That boy does get himself into some good scrapes, don't you know!' "

Everybody chuckled.

Everybody but Uncle Will, who'd been watching this exchange with a queer little smile. Jodi noticed him blinking tears from his eyes.

Uncle Will is beginning to change his mind about You, God, thought Jodi. She felt happier.

"What's in the envelope?" Mike asked.

She sat down on the sofa, the boys on either side, and tore the envelope open. A sheet of paper fell out. Mike peered over Jodi's shoulder and read aloud:

Dear Young Friends,

I want to thank you for your kindness to me. Your desire to restore the old cabin has given me much pleasure. I have a few of the household items we used when I was a small girl.

I kept my mother's sadirons and a few dishes, and some of the patchwork quilts she made, and the candlesticks my father carved. I have willed these things to the Bayside Historical Society. Perhaps they can be used in the cabin.

The package is for you, Jodi. You may do with it as you think best. May God bless all three of you. I remain always.

Your friend
Lucy Steincroft

Jodi folded the letter and slipped it back into the envelope. Everyone sat quietly for a few moments. Then Mrs. Marsh spoke.

"Mrs. Kratz said the funeral will be on Friday, the day after tomorrow. Would you three like to go?"

"I suppose we ought to," said Jodi. "But I still can't believe she's really gone."

Billy squirmed. "Open the package, Jodi."

She picked up the brown-paper wrapped parcel.

157

"It's heavy, but sort of floppy too," she said. "What do you suppose . . ."

She cautiously tore the paper away.

"It's a Bible!" she exclaimed.

"An old, *old* Bible," said Mike. The leather cover was worn with use. The yellowed pages were dog-eared and some were loose. Jodi carefully opened the cover.

"Oh, look!" She pointed to the first page, decorated with ornate gold scrolls and lettering. "It's a family register."

At the top of the page were written the names Julius A. Steincroft and Emma Barker and the date, June 21, 1900. "Those were Lucy's parents! Remember the newspaper notice? This must have been their wedding day."

Mike ran his finger down the page. "These other dates, right beneath the names. They must be their dates of birth and death."

"See, here's Lucy's name. Born August 16, 1901," Jodi murmured. She leafed through the pages, noting the tiny comments written in the margins.

"A whole lifetime of lessons learned from God's Word, right there in your hands, Jodi," said her mother.

"What are these?" As Jodi lifted the Bible from her lap, several faded photographs fluttered from between the pages.

The largest one showed an unsmiling woman in a high-collared white dress, standing behind a seated young man, both holding very still for the photographer. Jodi turned it over. " 'Julius and Emma Steincroft, June 21, 1900.' This was their wedding picture!"

"And look at this," said Billy. "It's Lucy!" A round-faced baby in a long christening gown stared out at them. Another photo showed a little girl of seven or eight. *Lucy Steincroft* was written on the backs of both pictures.

Jodi looked up. "I will keep these forever," she said. "Do you think we could have copies made to put in the cabin?"

"I'm sure we could," said her father. "Maybe we could even find another old Bible to put with the pictures, to show visitors that God's Word was important to the early settlers."

That night Jodi set the photos on the top shelf of her bookcase. She put the Bible next to Lottie on the nightstand. "Whenever I open this Bible," she told herself, "I'll remember Lucy."

Mrs. Marsh drove the cousins to the funeral home on Friday afternoon. Lucy's body lay on the pale blue satin of the open casket, like a fragile china doll, Jodi thought. Her gnarled hands were folded on her bosom, white hair smoothed neatly and a peaceful little smile on her lips. Jodi had dreaded that moment, but when she saw Lucy, she felt strangely comforted.

She thought of that feeling as they drove away after the funeral. "She looked—happy, Mom. Do you think she is?"

"Oh, I know she's happy! She's with the God she loved."

Jodi remembered Lucy's words, "Death is a door." On the other side of that door lay the beautiful home Jesus went to prepare for those who love Him. Someday, she would meet Lucy there.

But for now, there was the cabin project to look forward to, and more summers of adventure.

"Lucy, you won't be forgotten," Jodi whispered.